DRAGON'S BREATH

Books by Barry Smith

HISTORICAL NOVELS

The Kimberley Trilogy
For Freedom's Cause
Battle for the North
Kimberley Kill

Victoria's Twins —
The Rise of Manchester and Melbourne

ACTION-ESPIONAGE THRILLERS

Terror Trails
Dragon's Breath

DRAGON'S BREATH

BARRY SMITH

Dragon's Breath

Published by Barry Smith

First published 2020

© 2020 Barry Smith

 A catalogue record for this
book is available from the
National Library of Australia

978 09871779 4 0 (pbk)
978 09871779 5 7 (ebk)

Designed and typeset by Blue Wren Books
Printed by Ingram Spark

faceboook.com/BarrySmithWordSpinner

DEDICATION

In memory of my late wife, **Pat**, who always encouraged me to write, tolerated my creative madness and believed in my dream of becoming a published writer, even if I had to do it myself.

Remembering my dear friend, **Howard**, who did so much to help me smooth off my youthful rough edges, introduced me to Greece, France, London's East end and its riverside pubs. My boss and sidekick in swinging sixties London, he was always sensitive to my need for companionship to dispel youthful loneliness and have fun.

Not forgetting **Ken Siddons**, my mentor and Church Lad's Brigade Captain, who kept me off the Manchester streets, as a lad, and who is the inspiration for the fictitious Ken of the novel.

To my dear Brother **Charles** and his clergy wife, **Irene** who have bravely coped with significant health challenges during the year. All the best to them for a healthier future from here on.

ACKNOWLEDGEMENTS

I was somewhat inspired in choosing the focus of this novel by the vain attempt of the writer Erskine Childers to warn an under-armed Britain of the danger posed by the possibility of a German invasion, on the eve of WW1.

Robert Erskine Childers DSC was an English-born Irish writer who sought to warn Britain about the danger of Germany's military build-up and capacity for invading England before WW1, through writing his very influential novel '*The riddle of the sands*'. Churchill, then First Lord of the Admiralty, although hostile to spending money on armaments at the time, later gave the book the credit for persuading public opinion to fund vital measures against the German naval threat.

He went on to serve with distinction in the war including at Gallipoli. It is ironic that having supplied German guns in 1914 to the Irish Volunteers, who used them to attack British troops during the Easter Rebellion, he was arrested during the Irish Civil War, in 1922, by the then Irish government and executed by firing squad in Dublin. Ever the quixotic, romantic, before his execution he shook hands with the firing squad. His final words, spoken to the firing squad, were: "Take a step or two forward, lads, it will be easier that way."

MY BOOKS

A word of advice and caution to prospective readers of my books.

At all times I seek to inform and entertain, without being fanatical or preachy. My books fall into two main categories, according to their intended readership.

Historical novels

They aim to tell a story, based broadly, on historical fact and by adding a fair degree of imagination and literary licence, inform readers about events, actions, people and places — especially in an Australian context, through which fresh, light is shone on significant past events, in a painlessly, digestible, interesting and entertaining style.

For readers with a broad interest in domestic and international history and geo-politics and, who are curious enough, to wonder, *What, really/might have happened?* And to probe the reasons, *Why?*

Nowhere nearly as learned as Blainey, nor as dense, dark and philosophical as Mantel but, perhaps less polemical and certainly more fun than Fitzsimons. Their Australian-ness inspired by Shute and Upfield.

Perhaps, occasional recourse to a dictionary or Google required.

Action espionage thrillers

High octane, action packed, Australian, spy thrillers, unashamed to employ sex, violence and plentiful anti-politically correct, prejudice to fill in time on those long flights and provide good company in protracted, holiday idleness — yet spiced with a dash of serious intent.

Nothing like Le Carré, closer to Len Deighton, more credible than Bond. Most importantly, the plots, action and locations are Australian themed and located. Inspired more by Chandler, Corris and Temple than sad, lonely, Jack Reacher.

Those who still think it's 'our' ABC and read the *Guardian* every day, should approach with caution and handle wearing gloves.

No need for a dictionary or Google.

CONTENTS

Australia-China Context xiii
Notes on Dragons xvi
Uncommon word and place glossary xxiii
Abreviations xxviii

Dragon's Breath
  1. Back in harness 1
  2. Seductive Secrets 7
  3. The bigger picture 11
  4. Mending toxic teams 16
  5. Once an eagle-eyed swagman 19
  6. Chinese whispers 31
  7. In at the bounce 36
  8. Chinese walls 44
  9. Following the money 49
10. Back in the game 55
11. Plumbing the depths 58
12. Harvesting hearts and minds 65
13. Man on the run 72
14. Defence of the realm 78
15. Phantoms of the deep 89
16. Two-way spy 94
17. The dragon wakes 99
18. Stirring the dragon's brood 105
19. Blindsiding the dragon 111
20. Drawing the dragon's blood 116
21. Viral invaders 123
22. Fermenting false news 127
23. Scorched by the dragon 136
24. Dousing the dragon's fire 140

25.	Confronting the dragon	147
26.	Breaching the dragon's den	158
27.	Death to the dragon	165
28.	Fallout	169
29.	Epilogue	172

AUSTRALIA-CHINA CONTEXT

Why focus on China as a threat, when the west has at least tolerated, even facilitated and cheered on its economic rise and the benefit this has brought to its poor benighted people and the continued prosperity of its economic partners? To answer this question, we need to turn to history, a topic foreign to those born in and after the '60s and tainted by post-modernist teaching.

As the fortunate beneficiary of a rigorous English grammar school education in the '50s and '60s, topped off by tackling the History tripos at Cambridge university and coloured by my lived experience of China's doings over the last seven decades, I approach any assessment of modern China with extreme scepticism and cautious hope. China has often been the victim of malign foreign incursions, which its weak and corrupt Imperial structure was unable to resist. Its colonisation by European powers brought the pain of economic plunder, exploitation of its cheap labour and the curse of the drug trade, as well as the benefits of western technology — science, industrialisation, medicine, investment, telecommunications and infrastructure.

But again, as it began to rise, its progress was impeded once more by the invasion, depredations and atrocities inflicted on it by Imperial Japan during world war two. Its post war recovery was blighted by civil war, bringing the triumph of the European philosophy of Leninist Communism which, despite its unifying contribution to political and social change within China, became the malign force behind a new adventurism aimed at spreading this creed throughout its Asian neighbours. This led to major military conflict in Korea, Vietnam, Laos and Cambodia and ongoing terrorist activity to destabilise Malaya, Singapore and Hong Kong. My uncles fought insurgents in the Malayan jungles and at university I experienced the fury of anti-Vietnam war demonstrations

Adding to the pains this caused, the 'Stalinist' dictatorship of Chairman Mao and his Cultural Revolution killed millions of Chinese people and setback progress for a generation, until the adoption of unbridled Capitalism with a Socialist face, lifted millions out of poverty and saved the bacon of the communist party by avoiding the collapse that destroyed the Soviet Empire.

Correspondingly western attitudes to this new China became more accommodating, benefiting from selling into its vast market and shifting manufacturing there to exploit its cheap and disciplined labour force. It was believed that accepting China into the west's economic systems, such as the WTO and free trade agreements, would be the key to its evolution into a western style democratic society. Western political and business leaders became beguiled and seduced into believing that if tolerated, China would reform and become a benign collaborative global power.

But behind the mask of compliance with this pious hope, the Communist Party has proved to be intransigent in refusing to give up the reins of draconian power and embarked on the softer policy of hiding its relentless infiltration of western political and social systems and structures. Where it has been unable to persuade and seduce, it has used its economic power to buy its way into positions of influence and control, relying on the inherent greed of politicians and business leaders in the west and by filling the begging bowls of indebted, mendicant nations that have fallen prey to its alluring offers of aid and a road to prosperity.

Fortunately, recent Chinese Government initiatives and strategies have taken steps too far to be ignored by the more awake international observers. Just as Britain woke up, almost too late, to the threat of Imperial Germany's militarisation and again, when beguiled by Hitler into seeing him only as a bulwark against Stalin, almost entered into an unholy alliance, the scales are dropping from western nation's eyes and the tide has turned against the threat of the dragon. It is growing evidence of this denouement that has inspired this novel. Let us hope that the Chinese people can at last demand and enjoy a better course and turn their backs on the dangerous and misguided leaders at their ship's helm.

Barry Smith

NOTES ON DRAGONS

The Great Chinese Dragon – Many faces, many meanings

The Chinese reverence for dragons has evolved from totemic depictions of natural creatures to mythical animals with a multiplicity of characteristics and meanings.

The earliest known depiction of a dragon is a stylised C-shaped representation carved in jade. Found in eastern Inner Mongolia, it belonged to the Hongshan culture, which thrived between 4500 and 3000 BCE. It was almost always seen in a positive light and particularly associated with life-giving rains and water sources. Considered the most auspicious year sign, worn on the robes of emperors, depicted in the most precious materials from gold jewellery to jade figurines, and with countless references in literature and the performing arts, the dragon was everywhere in ancient China and looms as large today in the Chinese psyche.

It was said to dwell in water or clouds, was extraordinarily powerful and, when in flight, was accompanied by thunder and lightning — a 'serpent of the sky'. Descriptions gave it multiple attributes, sometimes with the body of a snake, the eyes of a rabbit, the belly of a frog, and the antlers of a deer. Other qualities of the dragon were that it could change its shape and size at will and disappear or reappear wherever it wished.

In China, the dragon was and is regarded as being a just and benevolent creature. It is for this reason they became associated with rulership and especially the emperors of China who, in their capacity as the holders of the Mandate of Heaven and as God's representative on earth, must always rule in a just and impartial manner for the good of all their subjects.

It was considered to be a lucky symbol-a provider of wind, rain, thunder, lightning and tornadoes. In rural communities, there was a dragon dance to induce the creature's generosity in dispensing rain and a procession where a large figure of a dragon made from paper or cloth spread over a wooden frame was carried. This is the origin of the ceremonial dragons that feature in Chinese, new year festivities. Alternatively, small dragons were made of pottery or banners were carried with a depiction of a dragon and written prayers asking for rain. Attendants would follow the procession carrying buckets of water and, using willow branches, they would splash onlookers and cry "Here comes the rain!".

The dancing processions had another handy purpose too, which was to ward off illnesses and disease, especially in times of epidemics. The link between dragons and rain, dancing and healing may all derive from shamanism, commonly practised in ancient China. The emperor was believed to be an incarnation of the supreme rain-bringing dragon. Then, in order to emphasise this auspicious association, he wore silk robes with dragon motifs exquisitely embroidered on them, sat on a throne with carved dragons, and had his palace adorned with architectural decorations showing dragons. The dragon associated with the emperor always had five claws to distinguish it from other lesser dragons who only had four claws. At the same time it came to symbolise the Imperial power.

The destructive, fire breathing dragon is more of a western perception and so in this novel it has taken on this fearsome form to represent the threat of the Chinese Communist Party, radiating from contemporary China, to disrupt and coerce democratic western societies, especially Australia.

The sun being chased by the dragon, thought to be responsible for a total eclipse — flag of the Chinese Empire under the Qing dynasty (1889–1912).

The Great English (Geordie) Dragon

The Lambton Worm Song

The song, based upon the Legend of the Lambton Worm, was written in 1867 by C.M. Leumane for a pantomime. The dialect is typical of the local area around Fatfield and Washington where I grew up. There is some translation on the right for the uninitiated.

—Audrey Fletcher, 2012

One Sunda morn young Lambton went
A-fishing in the Wear;
An' catched a fish upon *he's heuk*   (his hook)
He *thowt leuk*'t vary queer.   (thought looked)
But whatt'n a kind ov fish it was
Young Lambton cudden't tell—
He *waddn't fash te carry'd hyem,*   (could not be bothered to carry it home)

So he *hoyed it doon* a well   (threw it down)

Chorus
Whisht! lads, *haad yor gobs,*   (Listen! be quiet)
An' *aa'll tell ye aall an aaful* story,   (I'll tell you all an awful)
Whisht! lads, haad yor gobs,
An' Aa'll tel ye *'boot* the worm.   (about)

Noo Lambton felt inclined *te gan*   (Now ... to go)
An' fight i' foreign wars.
He joined a troop ov Knights that cared
For *nowther woonds* nor scars,   (neither wounds)
An' off he went te Palestine
Where queer things him befel,
An *varry seun forgat aboot*   (very soon forgot about)
The queer worm i' tha well.

(Chorus)

But the worm got fat an' *grewed an' grewed,*   (grew and grew)
An' grewed an aaful size;
He'd greet big teeth, a greet big *gob,*   (mouth)
An greet big goggly eyes.
An' when at *neets he craaled aboot*   (nights he crawled about)
Te pick up bits o' news,
If he felt dry upon the road,
He'd milk a dozen *coos.*   (cows)

(Chorus)

This *feorful* worm would often feed   (fearful)
On caalves an' lambs an' sheep,
An' *swally little bairns* alive   (swallow little children)
When they laid doon te sleep.
An when he'd eaten aall he cud
An' he had had he's fill,
He craaled away an' lapped he's tail
Ten times *roond* Pensha Hill.   (round)

(Chorus)

The news ov this *myest aaful* worm   (most awful)
An' his queer *gannins on*   (goings on)
Seun crossed the seas, *gat te* the ears   (soon … got to)
Ov brave an' *bowld Sor John.*   (bold Sir John)
So *hyem he cam an' catched* the beast,   (home he came and
    caught)

An' cut 'im in *twe* haalves,   (two)
An' that seun stopped hes eatin' bairns
An' sheep an' lambs an' caalves.

(Chorus)

So *noo ye knaa hoo aall the foaks*   (now you know how all the
    folks)
On *byeth* sides ov the Wear   (both)
Lost lots o' sheep an' lots o' sleep
An *leeved* i' mortal *feor.*   (lived … fear)
So *let's hev one te* brave Sor John   (let's have a drink to)
That kept the *bairns frae* harm,   (children from)
Saved coos an' calves by *myekin' haalves*   (making halves)
O' the *famis* Lambton Worm.   (famous)

(Chorus)

The Great (Brave) Welsh Dragon

Mametz Wood was the objective of the 38th (Welsh) Division during the First Battle of the Somme. The attack occurred between the 7th and 12th July 1916. On the 7th July the men were halted by machine gun fire before they reached the wood. Further attacks on the 8th July failed to improve the position. The Dragon commemorates this action and the sacrifice of the courageous Welshmen who died there and defiantly brandishes strands of broken barbed wire.

UNCOMMON WORD AND PLACE GLOSSARY

Barramundi (Barra) — A fish, native to Australia and the Indo-Pacific, barramundi proves to not only offer a desirable taste and culinary properties, it's packed with heart-healthy Omega-3s and is a hardy species that lends itself to farming without antibiotics or hormones.

Baron of Beef — A British meat choice, synonymous with any cut of beef that is well suited to roasting or braising such as top round, inside round, bottom round or the steamship round. Because top round is lean, the cut is considered a healthier choice.

Bobby Sands — Robert Gerard Sands was a member of the Provisional Irish Republican Army who died on hunger strike while imprisoned at HM Prison Maze in Northern Ireland. Sands helped to plan the 1976 bombing of the Balmoral Furniture Company in Dunmurry, which was followed by a gun battle with the Royal Ulster Constabulary.

Cislunar Space — *Cislunar* (Latin for on this side of the moon) Lying between Earth and the moon.

Éire — The modern Irish Éire evolved from the Old Irish word Ériu, which was the name of a Gaelic goddess. Ériu is generally believed to have been the matron goddess of Ireland, a goddess of sovereignty, or simply a goddess of the land.

Fenians — The Fenian Brotherhood (Irish: *Bráithreachas na bhFíníní*) was an Irish republican organisation founded in the United States in 1858 by John O'Mahony and Michael Doheny. It was a precursor to Clan na Gael, a sister organisation to the Irish Republican Brotherhood. Members were commonly known as "Fenians".

Five Eyes Alliance — The *Five Eyes* (FVEY) is an intelligence *alliance* comprising Australia, Canada, New Zealand, the United Kingdom and the United States. These countries are parties to the multilateral UKUSA Agreement, a treaty for joint, cooperation in signals intelligence.

The Fourth Estate — The term Fourth Estate or fourth power refers to the press and news media both in the explicit capacity of advocacy and implicit ability to frame political issues. Though it is not formally recognised as a part of a political system, it wields significant indirect social influence.

Ganbei — The default toast in China is *ganbei* (sounds like: "gon bay") which literally means "dry cup." And unlike in the West, you'll be expected to empty your cup after each toast given, or at least give it your best effort.

The Kimberley — is Western Australia's sparsely settled

northern region, three times larger than England and with a population of less than 40,000. It's known for large swaths of wilderness defined by rugged ranges, dramatic gorges, semi-arid savanna and a largely isolated coastline. The mostly unsealed (unpaved) Gibb River Road runs 660km through the region's heart, passing by Windjana Gorge National Park, which has towering limestone cliffs and pools where freshwater crocodiles gather.

Loyal Wingman, unmanned drone — is 38-foot-long (11.5 metres) and with a range of 2,000 miles (3,218.6 kilometres), uses artificial intelligence to fly independently, or in support of manned aircraft, while maintaining safe distance between other aircraft. This drone is able to engage in electronic warfare as well as intelligence, reconnaissance and surveillance missions and swap quickly between those roles.

Moscow Rules — The Moscow rules are rules-of-thumb said to have been developed during the Cold War to be used by spies and others working in Moscow.
- Assume nothing.
- Never go against your gut.
- Everyone is potentially under opposition control.
- Do not look back; you are never completely alone.
- Go with the flow, blend in.
- Vary your **pattern** and stay within your cover.
- Lull them into a sense of complacency.
- Do not harass the opposition.

Norforce — The NORFORCE is an infantry regiment of the Australian Army Reserve. Formed in 1981, the regiment is one of three Regional Force Surveillance Units employed in surveillance and reconnaissance of the remote areas of Northern Australia.

Porton Down — British Government's centre for research into the world's most deadly pathogens — diseases that can kill you.

The Purnululu National Park — is located in the state of Western Australia. It contains the deeply dissected Bungle Bungle Range composed of Devonian-age quartz sandstone eroded over a period of 20 million years into a series of beehive-shaped towers or cones, whose steeply sloping surfaces are distinctly marked by regular horizontal bands of dark-grey cyanobacterial crust. They look uncannily like row after row of Darth Vader helmets.

Red Dog — The legend is based on a true story of a Kelpie/cattle dog cross (sometimes called a Red Kelpie) who lived from 1971 until November 21, 1979. Red Dog was well known for his travels through the Pilbara region of Western Australia.

Strine (Australian English) — *Strine* is a result of speaking very quickly and running the words together. Examples include: "avva nysweegend" which translates to 'have a nice, weekend; caused by speaking through closed lips, to keep the flies out

Wandjina — The Wandjina are cloud and rain spirits from Australian Aboriginal mythology that are depicted prominently in rock art in Australia. Some of the artwork in the Kimberley region of Western Australia dates back to approximately 4,000 years ago

Yabbies — The common yabby is an Australian freshwater crustacean in the Parastacidae family. It is listed as a vulnerable species of crayfish by the International Union for Conservation of Nature, though wild yabby populations remain strong, and have expanded into new habitats created by reservoirs and farm dams.

ABREVIATIONS

AAP — Australian Associated Press is an Australian news agency. It was established by Keith Murdoch in 1935. Its journalists work in bureaus in all states and territories of Australia.

ASIS — *Australia's* overseas secret intelligence collection agency. Its mission is to protect and promote *Australia's* vital interests.

ASIO — Australian Secret Intelligence Organisation is Australia's national security agency responsible for the protection of the country and its citizens from espionage, sabotage, acts of foreign interference, politically motivated violence, attacks on the Australian defence system, and terrorism

CCP — Chinese Communist Party.

CSIRO — The Commonwealth Scientific and Industrial Research Organisation is an Australian federal government agency responsible for scientific research. CSIRO works with leading organisations around the world.

MCC — The **Melbourne Cricket Club** is a sports club based in Melbourne, Australia. It was founded in 1838 and is one of the oldest sports clubs in Australia.

MCG — Melbourne Cricket Ground.

PLA — People's Liberation Army, China's military forces.

SAS — The Special Air Service is a special forces unit of the British and Australian Armies. The SAS was founded in 1941 as a regiment, and later reconstituted as a corps in 1950. The unit undertakes a number of roles including covert reconnaissance, counter-terrorism, direct action and hostage rescue.

DRAGON'S BREATH

1
BACK IN HARNESS

Along the Murray River

Swimming strongly against the current and feeling his way along the riverbed was the diver's only way of detecting his quarry in the swirling, murky water. It was icy, cold and exhausting work. But diving for antique bottles, chucked over the stern of Murray river paddle steamers by well-oiled, pioneer, passengers, was sufficiently addictive to keep him at it, regardless of the cold and dark.

But it was getting late and despite the paucity of his catch, he was too tired and cold to stay down much longer until, he bumped against what felt like a floating bundle of rags. He decided to surface and see what he had caught. It was too heavy to swim up with and he sent it to the surface, tied to his bottle bag line.

His companions pulled the bundle into the support boat. The smell was awful, and they reeled back in horror, when closer inspection revealed a bloated, human body, dressed in a suit and raincoat. When the police came, they were equally shocked by this unexpected discovery.

"It's not often we get one like this, chief. He's too well dressed for a careless holiday maker, so it's unlikely to be an accidental drowning."

"Too right sergeant and before we get ahead of ourselves, we will have to wait for an autopsy, to establish whether we have a case of suicide or foul play, on our hands."

Melbourne, Lygon Street

Ken Eliot dusted down his office chair, tipped the dead flies from his in-tray and filed a wadge of bills in the 'forget about it', bottom draw of his desk. He kept the blinds closed to back up the air conditioner's losing battle with the heatwave scorching the street outside.

Ken's collar chafed his raw tan and his shoes pinched after weeks of going barefoot and living in shorts and singlets on Gippsland's ninety-mile beach. He was not the only bread winner suffering the post-Christmas, back-to-work, syndrome, in the dog days of January, when Melbourne emulated Athens in August, sweltering through days of thirty degrees or more. Lightly clad tourists packed Lygon Street's pavement cafés and though Alfonso's kept a reserved table for him, he favoured the comparative cool of his office on a day likely to hit forty.

His answering machine messages urged him to call his bank manager, accountant and sundry creditors, but there was no sign of client enquiries offering the prospect of paid employment. Such was the consultant's financial drought during the over-long break, resulting from the calamitous, coincidence of Christmas and summer holidays. At least his colleagues had not used all of the coffee capsules, kept in the lunchroom cupboard and a shot of the pure, Jamaica Blue grind worked its uplifting magic on his depressed spirit.

If he were Chandler's Philip Marlow or Corris's Cliff Hardy, facing the same bleak prospects, the entry of a blonde in shapely widow's weeds, offering him a richly paying assignment he couldn't and absolutely wasn't going to refuse, would change the colour of this gloomy day.

A sharp rap on his door raised hopes, soon dashed by the uninvited entrance of a tall, dark, athletic, man, whose Henry Buck's suit, stylishly barbered hair and neatly trimmed beard, attested to his sophisticated tastes and the wherewithal to buy and enjoy them. He mangled Ken's outstretched hand and greeted him with a native sarcasm that spoke of familiarity and a reluctant degree of respectful, regard.

"G'day Ken. Good to see at least one bastard back in harness, working to support my leisured life. What's up, fishing for custom more enticing than pursuing beach bunnies?"

"Hi Jack. Can't expect someone still suckling on his golden christening spoon to appreciate the genteel poverty of a consultant at this time of year. How about you — barred from the Melbourne Club, not selected to a polo team?"

"OK. OK. Let's call it a draw and if you make me one of those enticing coffees and allow me to light a cigar, I will tell you why it is in your interest to hear what I have to say."

Though raised in the country, Jack had the appropriate pedigree to qualify as a member of the Melbourne establishment. Educated at Melbourne Grammar and University, he was called to the bar and made the required pilgrimage to London working in the law and learning the journalistic and editorial trades on a Murdoch tabloid.

As the scion of a fifth-generation rural newspaper dynasty, he was appointed editor of their leading journal and became well versed in the Machiavellian ways of bush political parties and country politics. At the same time, he continued to be somewhat of a creative dreamer and loved to go bush, fishing for barramundi and dodging crocodiles on remote Kimberley beaches, leaving his more pragmatic brother to get the papers printed and distributed. Ken had worked with the family business and this had led to an occasional catch-up lunch, when Jack was in town, but that he had come to Ken's office, without notice and on such a stinking hot day, suggested he had more serious and hopefully, rewarding business to discuss.

In typically editorial fashion Jack got to the point and his story both intrigued and fascinated Ken.

"As you probably know from our history Ken, the country life is neither as quiet nor crime and violence free as myth would have it. Since before federation, landowners and bush workers have often been in strife and with post war migration, we took in some bad practices from impoverished parts of Europe-you may remember the murder of Donald Mackay in the Riverina, for blowing the whistle on suspected drug- dealing, mafia. Hence, we don't get too excited about occasional flare ups of violence or criminality, but a recent run of seemingly unrelated incidents, up our way, has me worried. The main dairy plant has been sabotaged beyond repair, the fruit packing plant, handling China exports, has burnt down and our leading winery has lost a vintage due to the outbreak of a blight that has not been seen here since before the turn of the century."

"That's serious Jack but if nobody was killed or injured and there is no obvious connection, could you be expressing premature alarm?"

"You are right Ken and that's what I thought when our editor proposed writing a speculative article about these incidents and the possibility of a common link or perpetrator. But when he received a bullet in the mail, after we printed his editorial, I really began to take this seriously and brought in the police. They were somewhat sceptical because of the absence of hard evidence and they suggested we beefed up security on our plant and offices. So, I sent the editor on leave to spend some recovery time with relatives down in Adelaide."

"So why are you here and how could I possibly help?"

"Firstly Ken, we value the work you have done for us and appreciate your discretion. Nobody has been indiscreet, but I have picked up nods and winks about why you might have gone home, why you have come back and why both police sources and the more secret types speak very highly of you. In short we believe you could offer us more than just change consulting and most importantly you are trusted by my father and brother."

"You will appreciate Jack that I cannot comment on what you have heard about my recent, past but I am interested in hearing how you think I could help."

"The key things that make you suitable for what I will propose are that you are an outsider from the city and a Pom with no history of involvement in country business, life or politics. You are an astute, listener and would easily pass off up our way as someone interested in learning more about bush history, perhaps in preparation for a book-maybe a novel. As our workshop was held in Melbourne there is little likelihood of anyone in town knowing of any connection between us. You are the ideal person therefore to come up and fossick around with no apparent plan and see if you might pick up some clues, that are escaping those of us who are perhaps too close to everything. What do you think?"

"I must admit Jack that you have intrigued me and a cash injection, at the moment, would be more than welcome. More than that I have equal regard for you, your family and employees and would love to help you get to the bottom of these incidents. Furthermore, I always welcome the chance to get away into the bush, especially when being paid for it. I must insist however, because of what you hinted at about my relationship with authorities, I would have to have the blessing of Victoria Police before I took this work on."

"Thank you Ken, your agreement is greatly appreciated and will be adequately rewarded. I must confess however that before seeing you I cleared my lines with the police, and they were both agreeable and very, supportive of your involvement. They would like you to drop into their city headquarters, as soon as possible, to be briefed on the general background and to agree the appropriate ground rules.

Now having settled that how about I treat you to lunch at Donnini's — they still have the best home-made pasta in Melbourne?"

2
SEDUCTIVE SECRETS

Melbourne, Police Headquarters

The modern police headquarters that had succeeded the grim old Russell Street fortress, was all reflective glass, stainless steel and was flooded with shimmering, daylight. Having ascended to the tenth floor and followed the reception sergeant's direction to turn right along the corridor, Ken was surprised to see that he was entering an area assigned to the Australian Federal Police. He had assumed that a domestic criminal matter would be the province of Victoria Police rather than the Feds and wondered whether he had misunderstood the directions. But, sure enough, room 1002, to which he had been sent, was on his right.

A female constable greeted him at a reception desk and after relieving him of his pass led him to a small inner room where two, very capable looking, federal cops, required him to submit to both electronic and manual security checks. This was way over the top for a local police matter and he began to wonder what he had got himself into.

"All clear sir. The commander is waiting for you in his office."

The uniformed Commander was polite and friendly without crossing the line into over familiarity.

"Good morning Mr Eliot. I am sure you have lots of questions, especially about why you are to be briefed in Federal Police offices, but if you will be a little more patient the people who are waiting for you in my conference room will reveal all you need to know."

Ken followed him into the adjoining room and closed the door behind him then just as he was to exclaim at sight of a familiar figure, strong, tensile, fingers, with steel-sharp nails, locked onto his throat and a soft, feline voice warned him, "These really are claws of steel Ken and as I warned you, before you left Manchester, they are fit to scar anyone who does not take me sufficiently seriously!"

Freeing himself from the relaxing grip, he spun round and opened his arms to embrace and accept a tender kiss from the lovely woman behind him.

"Kat, you bitch. You frightened me to death and why are you in Melbourne without warning me? As for you George, such skulduggery is not unexpected, but even the subterfuge in getting me along here is a bit low and I've a good mind to walk out now and take Kat to lunch, leaving you to stew in your own juice."

"Now Ken you know that we have always approached you in unconventional ways, because you always expect to be persuaded rather than dragooned into working for us and I have no problem with your swanning off with Kat, as she can brief and proposition you as well, if not better, than I can. Also, you are more likely to pay heed to what she will tell you rather than hearing it from me. Alright, at least shake my hand and then bugger off and have a good, but not too expensive, lunch on us. I'll see you later to conclude the formalities."

The heat wave continued, and they chose to eat in the RACV club's dining room because of its superior air conditioning and the discreet seating arrangements that precluded eaves droppers.

"I have so many questions Kat, but first-of-all, why are you here? How can MI6 spare you, with so much going on in the UK and Europe? Don't you remember our agreement that you would warn me if you were heading home?" Holding up her hand to stem his over-eager enquiries and raising a glass of cold, straw-coloured Barossa Chardonnay, she saluted him and began to answer his questions.

"G'day Ken. You don't know how good it is to be with you again. Firstly, I am here because I want to be. I have been released by MI6 and have accepted an informal contractual arrangement to take on occasional assignments for George at ASIS. How can this be when I was so keen to continue working with them?-I'm afraid my mother had a stroke and as dad was not coping too well, I decided to return and be closer by to care for them and ensure they have the best support arrangements in place. In addition, I hoped there might be a chance to team up with you again, as we did against the Russians and those IRA bastards, who tore out my fingernails, leaving me with these artificial, steel, talons. Now, let's order, those Coffin Bay oysters are to die for after the poor English excuses for sea food, served up in London."

As they ate their way through the succulent oysters and rich, aromatic, slices of pork loin, Kat briefed him on why he was being approached and why she and ASIO were involved.

3
THE BIGGER PICTURE

After lunch, they retired to a private meeting room, where Kat continued to fill Ken in on the bigger picture and to answer his queries.

"You probably don't appreciate how well-connected Jack and his family are. They have been heavily involved in National Party affairs going back before Black Jack McEwen's time and their stable of country papers is an influential and respected voice in the old, moneyed heartlands of Victoria. That's how we became aware of these significant, but seemingly unrelated episodes, and whilst we still have not detected either obvious links or foreign hands at work, the sending of the threatening bullet and now, I am sorry to tell you, the death of the editor under very suspicious circumstances, it has certainly become a police matter. Our political masters have suggested we give it the once over, if only because the industries involved are significant exporters to our new friends in China and donate heavily to the coalition parties."

"If such a run of sabotage had occurred back in the early sixties the focus would have been on the Italian Mafia, which dominated the drug trade in the NSW Riverina district. A whistle blower was murdered, and his body never found. But it is hard to finger a similar influence today. Any further leads or clues I have not yet heard about?"

"No, Ken. You know as much as us. That's why we want you to go up country and perform your listening act. You are known to be a keen outback traveller and camper and you have dabbled a bit in writing. It's been suggested that Jack's papers will print a brief bio about a visiting Pommy writer from Melbourne who will be coming to tour the district, researching for a travel book and maybe even a novel. This should gain you an entrée to the squattocracy and acceptance in the bar of most pubs. You see Ken it's the same old story. These long-established communities are pretty wary when it comes to city types and even more so when real foreigners come along. But tight as they are, someone in the community will know something about what is going on, behind the scenes and what we need is the loose thread that will unravel the jumper-just as I did in St Petersburg. It may only be a matter of commercial rivalry, but right now we have nothing that provides a motive or points to serious, maybe international, criminal forces."

"If I agree to this what will your role be if any?"

"Similar to our approach was in Spain and Russia, only this time you will be the tethered goat and I will be the big game hunter backing you up when the tiger attacks."

"You sound so encouraging. But what if the tiger strikes too early, as the IRA did in Melbourne-which cost you your fingernails and almost took your life?"

"I'm sure George will be prepared to contract your former special forces mates and, like last time in Albert

Park, they could provide all the supporting firepower we are likely to need. Also, they are off the books, their actions are deniable, and they can be dumped when the job is done."

"Looks like I need to get along to the All Nations, in Richmond, again and buy Pete a drink. He took it very personally that the IRA was able to abduct and torture you and he will be delighted at the prospect of working with you again."

"Well, here's to us again Ken."

The formalities were soon settled with George. Ken was sworn in and the newspaper article suggested that the writer might also require the occasional help of a woman photographer and researcher come down from Sydney. Then, quite coincidentally and fortuitously, an international food packing company, with farms and a processing plant in the area, engaged Ken to advise them on a major organisational change, which required evidence gathering interviews with a range of employees, from top management to shop floor.

Vic rail trains were just as streamlined as any in Europe but that's where the comparison ended. Despite considerable political hype and expenditure, journey times into the city had been reduced by a mere fifteen minutes and these 'faster' trains only ran in the narrow morning and evening commuter windows. It mattered little to Ken, as he had no deadline to meet, and the delightful Victorian charm of the station at which he alighted reminded him that sophistication didn't stop at the end of suburbia. The distance into town was short enough that he chose to walk and shouldering his backpack luggage he set off at a leisurely pace-much to the disappointment of the Sikh driver at the head of the taxi queue. A long macchiato at a high street café further confirmed this town was no 'hicksville' and set him up for his first stop at the newspaper office.

The acting editor welcomed him and, as instructed by his boss, suggested Ken might like to take up a pre-paid room at a central, colonial-style hotel, where most of the town's raconteurs and gossips drank and especially the journalistic fraternity and their politician prey.

The mood in the office was sombre and respectful of the funeral of their late editor, which was to take place in the next few days. The pub was typical of its era-big and bold, with lots of wrought iron trimmings and a wrap-around balcony, which had served as a grandstand, in the days when horse races used the high street as the finishing strait.

The bar was dark and cooled to some extent by electric ceiling fans. At least it had forsaken the choking fug of tobacco smoke but not the smell which had impregnated the soft furnishings. It was sufficiently after lunch to be underpopulated and only a few hard drinkers eked out their daily grog addictions. There was little to be learned from this crowd, but he made himself known, bought a few drinks and thereby let it be known that he had arrived and why he was there. He allowed the local characters to regale him with their favourite myths and legends and at least gained an early insight into the town's social strata, who was who and which horses were sure winners at the upcoming picnic races. The bar maid proved to be a useful judge of which, if any, of these informants had anything true or worthwhile to say.

It was perhaps a little over the top, but he had agreed with George that communications would be subject to secret intelligence disciplines and the assumption was made that telephone and email connections might be compromised. For all but the most urgent messages he used Australia Post's guaranteed next day delivery and his first report confirmed that it worked.

4
MENDING TOXIC TEAMS

Business in the bush

Mending toxic teams was a core part of his consultancy work and Ken approached the assignment with his usual open-minded scepticism. His initial briefing had been by the company's HR Director in Melbourne. The problem was said to be the overbearing behaviour of the plant general manager. After a further session with the manufacturing director it seemed the problem might be more than just the leader's failings and additionally the dysfunctional behaviour of his team.

He had contracted to interview all the players, including the recalcitrant boss and this gave him an immediate opportunity to gauge the mood and opinions of the managers in a comparable factory to those which had suffered sabotage. As usual there was just as much friction between the team members as their disaffection for their boss. It never ceased to amaze him that the old police routine of interviewing suspects and witnesses, separately, unearthed more common opinions than contradictions and what stood out in this case, was their unanimous unease with the style of their Chinese, Finance Manager and her superior attitude to all her colleagues.

It was little wonder that this hard-driving, exceptionally bright and qualified accountant, a migrant from Malaysia, who had battled through Monash university, financed by night work, shot up the corporate ladder, stepping on the fingers of lesser men, should discomfort her essentially country-bred, time serving, colleagues.

She was a delight to interview, after the evasive and reticent men and certainly didn't hold back in her assessment of their strengths and weaknesses, with which Ken was readily able to concur without appearing to collude with her. But despite her sparkle and sharp, articulate delivery, he detected a cold and ruthless streak that would need to be teased out and addressed during the forthcoming workshop.

From the others he learned that her forcefulness and ambition didn't stop within the factory gate and that she was already a leading light in the Chinese community. She had joined the National Party which gave her entrée to the landowners and business leaders and the Chinese restaurant run by her husband and family gave her many contacts in the wider community.

The old boys in the pub had spoken of the Chinese Australians in the town who were the ancestors of the nineteenth century prospectors that had walked to Ballarat and Bendigo from Robe in South Australia, where they had disembarked to avoid the prohibitive Victorian Government tax on incoming Chinese. In recent years as Communist China had opened-up and shown interest in Australia's world class food and mineral exports, an additional but lesser number of skilled Chinese technicians and managers had taken up residence. It was these newcomers who worked hardest to keep Chinese culture alive and always expressed their pride in the rise of their motherland. Madame Wu was amongst the foremost of this diaspora.

The plant manager was at the other end of the spectrum. Like Jack, the descendent of early farming pioneers and a mover and shaker in the Anglo-Celtic, Australian bush aristocracy. Tom Clancy was shrewd enough to know his confronting style rubbed his team up the wrong way and he valued Wu's skills and commitment to the business so highly, that he tolerated the extent to which she was a disruptive influence, even when her quick and penetrating analysis shot down many of his seemingly creative but unsound initiatives

Ken's feedback from the interviews assured the team members that he had teased out the key issues, that he was professional and that the accuracy and honesty of his summations proved he was not their boss's puppet. Tom took the implied criticism of his performance on the chin and agreed with the others that they should proceed to a residential weekend workshop to address their differences. Before Ken left, Tom thanked him for opening up the issues in an honest but indestructible way and invited him to come out to the family homestead for dinner on Saturday night.

5
ONCE AN EAGLE-EYED SWAGMAN

The homestead was a fine Victorian pile, whose grounds rolled down to the banks of the flood-swollen Murray river. The quality of cars parked at the front spoke of well-heeled guests and a walking advertisement for R M Williams' stockman's gear greeted Ken and directed him to the rear, river-front veranda, where guests were hopping into pre-dinner drinks and snacks, hot from a barbecue manned by a town chef. The patriarch of the manufacturing group dynasty greeted Ken and thanked him for coming.

"G'day Ken. Very, good to meet you and delighted to hear you are planning to write a book about our area. There is too much focus on Melbourne nowadays and I hope you will highlight the importance of our food bowl which feeds not only our city friends but also, is such a vital export earning industry, now that mining is in the doldrums."

"The pleasure is all mine Mr Clancy. It's good to be a guest in your fine home and I am looking to you to introduce me to those who can fill me in on the history and stories of the region."

"I can certainly do that and let's start with Senator Tom

Baker here who is our leading politician and a minister in the state government."

"Welcome to country Victoria Ken. You have chosen well in making us the background to your book. We have a varied history and play a vital role in creating the country's wealth. Be sure to come and see me either here or at Parliament House if I can do anything to help you uncover useful information and sort the facts from the myths: especially those regarding the Chinese who are playing a key role in bankrolling the growth of our export businesses."

As Ken thanked him, the dinner gong sounded, and everyone moved into a spacious dining room where large round tables were set with central, lazy susans, individual bowls and chop sticks. The meal was excellent and was provided by the leading Chinese restaurant managed by Madam Wu's husband. Whilst he was careful to play a backroom role in the kitchen, she was out front taking credit for the delicious catering.

Ken made many useful contacts during the evening for later reference but one, in-particular who was recommended but not present, intrigued him most. A fascinating, almost legendary character, known locally as the Wombat, lived in the bush, managing to sustain himself with minimal external help. On occasions he called at bush-edge properties to trade with kangaroo meat and possum furs and do chores in return for essential supplies. He only came into town when medical treatment, such as dentistry, was needed. It was believed that some perceived disgrace had caused him to flee from the town, at least twenty years ago and despite living a self-sufficient life, alone in the bush, he was said to be clean, healthy, sound in mind and with encyclopedic, knowledge of the flora and fauna of the forest tracts along the river.

On the following day, a summons to the police station revealed the autopsy finding that the editor had been murdered. A microscopic needle prick in his skin and the presence of a narcotic in his blood stream suggested that he had been rendered unconscious before he was drowned in the river. Also, an eyewitness had seen men throw something into the river, up-stream of where he had been found. The bushman had been collecting firewood for his camp and although his view was in bright moonlight, they were too far away for him to identify them.

It was time for Ken to call on the Wombat.

Somewhere in the bush

The police advised him that they would send word that he wished to talk with the Wombat and assured him that he would never find him by blundering around in the bush. He had no fixed abode and was so skilled in hiding his tracks that only the most experienced aboriginal tracker could follow his trail. On the appointed day, Ken drove to a riverside clearing and as he stopped, turned off the engine and stepped out of the car, a tall man dressed in a worn, denim shirt and moleskin strides emerged from the surrounding trees. His thick head of iron grey hair and bushy beard were spotlessly, clean and his piercing blue eyes stood out in a face tanned to the consistency of sueded, leather. His hands were coarsened and calloused by work and his handshake almost caused Ken to wince with pain.

"You must be Ken. The Police say you need help in writing a book. So what do you want to know?"

"That's right but before we get to that it's my habit to have a cup of coffee at this time of day and as I have a fine espresso brew in my flask you might care to join me."

Wombat readily agreed and, taking his black and without sugar, asked Ken's permission to load up and light a well-worn and clearly much-loved pipe.

"I know that smoking is frowned upon and often restricted in cities but out here it helps keep off the flies and mosquitos at night."

Wombat was well versed in the history of this part of the state, suggesting that he had had a good education, before fleeing from so-called civilisation and, as an often unseen observer on the fringe of urban society, he had much to say about clandestine goings on that took place in the surrounding bush.

"I understand that politicians, newspapers and academics can tell you much about the history and current goings on here but what they miss is the view at ground level, the truthful, eye-witness of the common men and women, who work and live beneath the radar of these exalted ones. It was clear to me that the newspaper editor was murdered and but for my evidence the suicide conclusion might have gone through unchallenged."

"That's why I am talking to you. I want to really know who and what makes things work around here, where the "bodies" might be buried and who the real power brokers are."

"First, you have to separate assumed power from real power, which is often in the hands of people who don't care to use it. The local bigwigs and city councillors will tell you that they are responsible for comfortable living standards and full employment but it is the progressive farmers and vignerons who grow the green, clean, food products that the increasingly affluent Chinese will buy, at almost any price-such as baby formula milk powder-which ensures the safety of their children's diets. These people are not too fussed about who buys the fruits of their labour nor who owns the businesses that convert and export raw materials, as long as their lifestyles are preserved. It is those at the so called 'top' that compete, employing political and financial corruption and even violence, to secure more than their fair slice of the pie. You will need to tap into the basic social layer — what I call the real people — to find out what is actually going on."

"How do you suggest I do that?"

"I understand you are a management consultant as well as a writer. Use this work you are doing in the food company to talk to people on the shop-floor, as well as management. Come into the bush and I will introduce you to the small farmers, sub-contractors and the often, exploited itinerant workers who pick and pack the produce. Also, find a way into the local Chinese community-the old original Chinese population, whose ancestors came to dig for gold and stayed to cook and keep the gardens on the sheep and cattle stations. You can find them running small businesses and the take-away Chinese restaurants — less lavish than the one owned by Mr Wu. The cops can give you some names."

Driving back into town Ken admired the sporting facilities. There was an abundance of football grounds, tennis courts, cricket ovals and bowling greens, all with brand new architect designed pavilions and club houses. The civic swimming complex boasted outdoor and indoor fifty metre pools, as well as ancillary pools for water aerobics, water polo and children's play areas. This was sure evidence of local economic prosperity.

Ken thought better of going back to the police and being seen as too close to them. It was clear there were clues just below the town's seemingly placid surface and he chose to search for them by resuming his enquiries at the factory. In his own factory working days he had learned that the supervisory level people, rather than the management, engineers, accountants and lawyers, really ran the place and knew most about what was going on. The same was true of the company nurse, paymaster and switchboard operator. When Ken learned that the nursing sister came from his home city of Manchester, he knew that he had found a loose thread worth pulling at. Beryl not only came from the same suburb, where Ken had been born, but he had shared a primary school desk with her nephew.

She invited him to lunch with her and her friends in the factory canteen and chatting with the maintenance and production supervisors, as well as the warehouse foreman and paymaster, he learned far more in an hour than he had learned in over fourteen hours of interviews with management. In his weekly report to George he was able to describe the fragilities that belied the seemingly stable surface of the food exporter. Maintenance budgets had been pared to the bone, so that machinery broke down far too frequently and the boilers that powered the plant were way beyond their due safety overhauls. In the warehouse, inventories did not match the night shift despatch tallies and the paymaster believed that the unseasonably quiet labour relations were more due to donations being made to union branch coffers and by virtue of this into the campaign fund of one of the state's leading political parties.

Ken was awoken from a deep sleep by the wail of police and fire brigade sirens. Switching on the hotel room TV he saw the diminutive form of a well-known local reporter excitedly describing the explosion of a boiler at the factory which, fortunately, had not cost any lives but would shut the plant for months.

He chose to eat lunch at a small Chinese restaurant out of the town centre. The furnishings were tired, the menu plain and servings came all together on a plate with knife and fork and a whole sliced loaf to be shared amongst guests. A true adaptation of one cuisine to meet the rural customers tastes. The ancestral family of the owner had come to Australia during the gold rush in the eighteen fifties and though visually Chinese, he and his staff spoke only the purest, Strine.

Trade was slow and the proprietor was happy to drink tea with Ken and chat about the Chinese Australians history and place in the town.

"The best way to describe the Chinese position here is in three parts. There are those of us who came from gold prospecting families and have been assimilated into Australia over more than one hundred and fifty years.

There is a small but growing clutch of Chinese students who come to our rural university to qualify and, hopefully, find a way to win citizenship. Then there is the new cohort of wealthy, Chinese who have managed either to bring ill-gotten gains out of China to invest here in property and businesses or build new, prosperous, opportunities for their kids. Some of these are agents for Chinese state-owned businesses, seeking strategic footholds in Australian industries. There are tremendous and growing tensions between these three groups."

At this point the owner's wife joined them and with a conspiratorial look at her husband she began to tell their personal tale.

"Our oldest son qualified in finance at the university and was doing well in Melbourne where he worked for the HSBC bank. He was so well thought of that he was transferred to Hong Kong for a while, before returning here. We were so proud of him and glad for the extra income he provided to keep our restaurant afloat. Then he stopped calling us and coming home for weekends from Melbourne. It was only when his uncle called on him and told us he was being pressured by people in China to work here, on their behalf, in what appeared to be illegal ways, that we experienced the reach of the old country into our lives. What was even more frightening was the message delivered through a Triad gang, based on the Queensland Gold Coast, that we and our son would suffer if he did not cooperate."

"What did you do? Did you go to the police?"

"Before we could consider, our son saved us by taking his own life." At that she broke down and he left them sitting, holding hands and reliving the bitter depths of their grief.

On the way back to his hotel the post office called Ken to advise there was a package waiting for him there. It was a message from George requesting his immediate return to Melbourne for further briefing and urging him to take the five o'clock train.

Melbourne, ASIO HQ

George wasted no time in getting to the point. The people in the factory had been warned by the Finance manager not to speak to Ken, who was only to work with the management team and there had been an attempt to attack the Wombat which had been frustrated by his superior bush skills.

"Clearly your cover has been blown already Ken and when you return up country, which we want you to do, you will need some unobtrusive but effective protection. I have spoken with Pete and his former SAS colleagues and three of them will be going up tomorrow to join you and back you up, without indicating they have any association with you."

Ken thanked George and caught the next train back. He was not surprised the cover had lasted so little time in a bush community where everyone knew everyone's business. It was dark when he left the train and headed along a quiet lane, on the way to a safe boarding house run by a former Melbourne policeman. Prior to his briefing, he wouldn't have taken any notice of the two men approaching him along the lane. But now he was alert to any potential sign of danger.

Suddenly, the men produced lengths of metal pipe from under their coats and advanced on Ken, with the obvious intention of breaking every bone in his body. He had the advantage of carrying his Glock pistol but didn't want to create a major incident by shooting them in the street. He could not assess their relative fighting abilities at this distance and so chose to run away from them, enabling him to deal with them in turn, starting with the fleetest of foot.

He allowed them to close on him and coming to a cross street he turned sharp left and stopped ready to surprise them as they followed. The first attacker rounded the corner at full speed and was shocked to find Ken braced to take him on. His unarmed combat trainers in England had stressed the value of using an opponent's momentum to gain advantage and by simply sticking out his leg, Ken's trip sent his pursuer sprawling headlong into the road where he fell with a sickening thud. A follow up kick to the ribs made sure he would not get up in a hurry and Ken prepared to face the second attacker who had not yet arrived.

When he did not come, Ken went back into the lane wondering whether he had chosen to run away. But to his surprise he saw that the man was lying on the ground and writhing in agony. Had he tripped over something in the dark and broken a leg? Ken approached him cautiously until he saw the crossbow bolt protruding from his would-be assailant's thigh. He recognised the handiwork but before he could call out his thanks and invite his back-up to break cover, his hunch was confirmed by a voice from the shadows.

"G'day Ken. You OK? Looks like I got here just in time. But I figured you could handle the first one without my help."

"Kat, what the hell are you doing here?"

"Don't you mean, thank God you appeared just in time Kat?"

Ken didn't answer until he had called up a police patrol which carted the attackers away and then putting his arms around her, he kissed and hugged Kat and thanked her for evening up an unfair fight.

"What now?"

"I'm heading for my digs for the night and to think about what my next move should be."

"As I am staying at the same address Ken, I guess you mean, what both our moves should be."

Their digs were well appointed and even offered the luxury of a cast-iron, lion's claw-footed bath, which Ken was eager to soak in and reflect upon all that had happened that day. He was stretched full length beneath a foaming layer of bath salts when he felt the presence of another body in the bathroom.

"Shove up Ken, there's room for two and I could do with a spell of relaxation and sharing of our reflections on today's experience." Without further ado Kat discarded her bathrobe and joined Ken in the bath. Apart from the damage to her finger tips, Kat displayed a perfectly statuesque body-flat belly, pendulous breasts and pert nipples that invited nuzzling, which so aroused Ken that he had to take himself in hand to prevent his proud cock breaking through the sudsy surface and proclaiming his lust.

"Ouch, that's hot, typical bloody Mancunian's idea of a warm bath. Turn on the cold tap and tell me what you are thinking."

Their talk adjourned to his bedroom where they reprised the energetic and sensual coupling that they had last enjoyed in Spain.

In the morning they called into the police station to complete statements about the previous night's attack and learn what was known about the prisoners. The two men had turned out to be local thugs hired for the occasion. They were not very bright but smart enough not to reveal the identity of their employer, whose retribution they feared more than time in a jail cell.

The same lunchtime soaks propped up the bar of the hotel, but they did not welcome the arrival of Ken and Kat and were suddenly unable or unwilling to answer any more questions and their stories had dried up. It was clear that there was nothing further to be learned from the locals

6
CHINESE WHISPERS

Melbourne, ASIO HQ

"There is not much point in your hanging out in the bush Ken, now that your cover has been blown and I have called everyone together to review what we have found out and to decide our next course of action. I have spoken with the minister about the possible Chinese links and she has made it clear that whilst we are free to follow up leads that point in their direction, we must be mindful of Australia's delicate, diplomatic, trade and commercial, relationships with them."

"As first Secretary in the Department of Foreign Affairs I have been sent to this meeting to underline the caution that George has just counselled. We are straddling the barbed wire fence of keeping in the good books of both Washington and Beijing. As far as China is concerned-we have a free trade agreement, they are the biggest customer for our mineral and energy exports, they own some of our key companies-especially in agriculture and their students are a key revenue earner for our tertiary education programs. We receive most investment from US and British sources but, when these are insufficient for our needs, we are not averse to doing financial deals with

Beijing. It is vital that you are not too indelicate in your public enquiries."

Beijing, China, Ministry of Foreign Affairs

"The Foreign Minister looked pleased after today's meeting with the President."

"He had good cause. The One Belt One Road strategy is shaping up well, as it merges our global economic interests with our strategic aims. It is so simple and yet so audacious in that we are being allowed to pursue an Imperialist policy, not unlike that which served Britain so well in the 19th century. We are gaining increasing access, if not ownership, of critical resources such as minerals, energy and food, in third world and developing countries, as an alternative to our dependence on western suppliers. The gullible fools are even willing to help us finance our strategy and, by upsetting what they see as undesirable regimes in Sri Lanka, Myanmar, Zimbabwe, South Africa, Fiji, Turkey and even Russia, they open the door for us to step in and increase our influence.

The Pacific Islands are leaning towards us, greedy for our gold, and this could net us a naval base to threaten US interests, which the imperial Japanese failed to do. It is truly breath-taking General, and so much more effective than our past military adventures and proxy wars, that delivered so little."

"Yes, Minister. Despite our sacrifices, those ungrateful North Koreans and Vietnamese have never lived up to our expectations. But we need to go carefully, we cannot rely on the Muslims in Pakistan and Turkey and the Russians are always as much a threat as an opportunity.

The strategy seems to be developing theoretically but there are still some obstacles on the ground, and I am not just referring to the USA."

"Ah yes. The European Union is unpredictable and of course whilst not a strategic threat, Australia is a stumbling block. We are making progress in infiltrating their key industries. We have succeeded in gaining financial, ownership and positions of influence over their infrastructure, education and political systems, but they still cling to the US alliance and act as a hub for South East Asian resistance to our South China Sea and Pacific strategies."

"You are right about Australia. A strange hybrid country. They are last to adopt the most effective technologies and economic strategies necessary to surge ahead, but prefer to be first in social revolution and experiments which hold back and limit their prosperity. Whilst we have been successful in planting the seeds of a significant diaspora, in some cases, their unquestioning loyalty to our mother country cannot be guaranteed also, Australians are tight with the Americans and though their military is small, their fighting history is famous, as we learned in Korea and they could act as a trip wire to give the US forces time to react to our aggression. That is the problem with the corrupting influence of democracy."

"It is as well that those of us who have much to lose from the growing centralist power of our state are awake to these threats and are taking steps to secure our wealth and heritage. There will be more encouraging news of this at our special meeting this evening. I look forward to seeing you there and do be careful that you are not watched. The surveillance is getting as bad as it was in Mao's day."

Beijing, Hotel Conference Room

"Gentlemen, welcome to the China-Australia Friendship Group. You may be wondering why we are meeting in such a public venue. A gathering of such eminent people would readily gain the attention of our security agencies and so our holding this meeting here and under such an innocuous title, is a way of hiding in plain sight. Rest assured also that the room has been swept for bugs, mobile phones are being held at the reception desk and every attendee was scanned on the way in to ensure no recording apparatus has been carried into the room. I will now call on our chairman to bring us up to date about what is happening regarding our interests in Australia."

"You are familiar with our national government's Australia strategy and so I will confine myself to indicating the opportunities and risks that this entails. We have long supported tolerance of the Communist political system, as long as we and our families continued to be allowed to benefit from an unbridled capitalist approach to international commerce and personal wealth accumulation. We need to be concerned that the impending changes in our government system will threaten our freedom and that already some of our ventures and profits have been falling under the influence of so-called anti-corruption agencies.

Our response to increasing centralised, dictatorial, control is to infiltrate and influence Australia's laxly guarded business, financial, property and political party funding systems. In this we have been very, successful. We are the main purchasers of high-end property in major cities. We own and have financial interests in ports, mines, power generation, telecommunications and even in some defence industry suppliers. But despite our cautious incremental approach even the naïve Australian authorities have become awake to our increasing strategic presence. Tonight, I will outline what we are doing to protect and secure our presence and assets in Australia. Our wealth and liberties are at stake and our methods may have to be increasingly ruthless, even recruiting the services of our own criminal, triad connections there."

7
IN AT THE BOUNCE

Canberra, ASIS HQ

"As Foreign Affairs has revealed, we have a watching brief on the big Chinese moves to cement a presence here, such as their leasing the port of Darwin and their major investments in the Ord River region, cattle, dairy and energy industries. They are likely bidders for access to the 5G mobile phone spectrum and ownership of strategic gas pipelines. But these seemingly unrelated incidents in Victoria may prove to be a case study in how they plan to expedite their influence to attain a position of significant control.

If there is a Chinese hand orchestrating these recent outbreaks of commercial sabotage in Victoria and, I must say your work suggests it is very likely, we need to risk going to the source to prove our thesis and to see how it can be countered and frustrated. But how to do this under the strictures placed upon us by our Foreign Affairs masters?"

"I think I get the drift chief — it's not unlike the situation MI6 faced in using us to grub around in Europe and Russia in order to gather intelligence about terrorist intentions, without creating a diplomatic incident."

"Spot on Kat. Our people are too well known and followed everywhere. The possibility is to infiltrate new people unknown to Chinese security."

"A bit harder than in Europe and Russia where we at least looked racially, similar to our hosts but here, we have both physical as well as linguistic barriers to our anonymity. How do you propose we get over those?"

"By not pretending to be what you are not, Ken. An AFL sponsored exhibition match scheduled to showcase the game in Shanghai will be followed by a return match here in a few weeks and you, Ken and Kat, will be part of the crew supporting the Australian team. Your duties will not be too technical nor too arduous, thus allowing you to fish for contacts and information, that may identify the perpetrators of our problems. It is such a fringe event they will not see any security threat and as some of our footy supporters will be involved, it will be easy for you to hide in a crowd of Aussie barrackers."

"You had better introduce us to the club so that we can pick up the football lingo. I don't know about Kat, coming as she does from the state of running wrestling, but despite my time in Victoria, arial ping pong takes some getting used to."

The great beauty of Australian Rules Football is that it is an indigenous game that like the wine industry grew and evolved from imported root stock into a unique form that reflects the growth of Australia from the early nineteenth century to the present day. The leading clubs preserve a quaint language, traditions and values that are rooted in the history of Melbourne's inner city suburbs and it seemed to Ken that its populist origins made it a most appropriate vehicle for engaging with an even older, but autocratic China.

Melbourne, Pre-season training

"Bounce the ball Ken and give it a good thump-you're not playing rugby now."

Ken's lungs were on fire and had he been forced to do another lap of the oval, because of some basic fumble, he felt sure he would die. How could Caucasians survive such a hard training regime, in what for him was Mediterranean high summer? He had accepted the suggestion he become familiar with the game from the inside but had not expected to join in training with professional players. It was years since he gave up rugby and even so, the level of fitness required to play this game for four quarters seemed barely possible for a human being. It was alright for Kat-she was working with the back-up staff but hopefully, her laughter and ribald comments might soon be stifled by her having to get down and dirty with the newly formed women's team.

"Why are you doing this Ken. You're no spring chicken and you can still write about the game without trying to play it?"

"That's not the point coach. I pride myself on the authenticity of my books and the government will want me to cover the Melbourne game in a way that shows the best of Australian grit and endurance."

The ice bath and massage session ensured that he could at least walk after the training run and he was not alone in his agonies.

"How goes it Chow Lim, are you as sore as me?"

The Chinese Government representative to the Sino-Australian Friendship through Football committee, grinned and rolled his eyes.

"Very sore Ken, but not as bad as you, because I have been training for weeks here and in China. So, it has not been such a shock for me. But the heat takes some getting used to. It was much cooler when we played in Shanghai."

Ken had made a point of befriending Chow Lim, to the extent that he drank tea with him, and they dined together at Melbourne's most authentic Chinese restaurants.

"Apart from your duty as a party man to get behind this program, why do you seem so thoroughly keen to participate in such a gruelling sport?"

"At first it was just a duty and, as you say, very hard work but the more I have played and become familiar with its rules and the nature of the Australian players, I have come to see how its apparent chaos is an expression of a free and lightly regulated way of living."

"Better not let your party boss hear you talking like that."

"It's a very private observation and one that is in tune with how a less corrupt China would be. I only dare share such a feeling with a trusted friend."

Melbourne, Grand Hotel, Richmond

"You certainly demolished that Grand Parma, Ken. I must say the counter meals here are excellent."

"Yes George, they come out of the kitchen that services the main Italian dining room."

"When you two have finished drooling over the food and service can we get down to business."

"Point taken Kat. Ken has been telling me that he may be on the brink of a break-through in gaining the confidence of Chow Lim."

"Perhaps he was sending you a message but equally, he could be trailing a hook to catch you and expose your undercover role."

"I don't think so Kat, but it pays to be cautious and I will be careful to let him do all the running at this stage. All being well, he could be the entrée to those who are pulling the strings here."

Along the Darling

"Look before you step over a log. Snakes like to curl up there and don't walk under the River Red Gums. In this heat, the trees are apt to explode and the falling branches can kill."

This was the only survival advice given by the Wombat as he guided Ken and Chow Lim through the bush along the riverbank. The shimmering heat and lack of breeze necessitated a slow deliberate pace and breathing slowly through the mouth avoided the sting of over-heated droplets of moisture vapourising in their nostrils. A sudden gesture from the Wombat brought them to a halt and he pointed to a pair of foxes trotting across a clearing. The river was flush with tropical rain which had come down the Darling from the far north and staked-out lines, from both banks, trailed yabby traps into the stream.

On reaching the site of a ruined hut the Wombat prospected the nearby earth with a long steel probe and when it had penetrated some ten feet below the surface, the telltale chink of metal on glass confirmed he had struck the hidden treasure lode. The hut had been the home of a Chinese station cook and beside the remains of his garden was the former refuse dump which concealed generations of discarded bottles and hopefully some rare finds. Chow Lim had been delighted at the prospect of being guided into the bush and reconnecting with the archaeological evidence of his ancestral fellow countrymen. He needed no encouragement to take up a mattock and start to break open the hard, dry, surface of the site.

By the time they had taken a rest break for morning tea, the evidence of their exploration lay before them. Most of the bottles were of unremarkable, medicinal, soft drink and beer container varieties but the jewel in their midst was a whisky bottle embossed with an entwining thistle, proudly embracing its whole length.

"What a beauty, Wombat. I guess that would fetch a good price on the bottle exchange market."

"It certainly would Ken, but as Chow Lim sweated to dig it out, it is his to keep, as a symbol of his ancestors' contribution to the opening up of this land."

Chow Lim's inscrutable face broke into a great grin of happiness and he expressed his pride in the find.

"Although the goldfields Chinese were despised and did such lowly jobs, their domestic service was a vital comfort to the white settlers and the fruit of their gardens contributed greatly to their dietary health. Thank you both for bringing me here and allowing me to pay my respects. We are building a very, different China to-day, but we must not forget our past and especially the founding pioneers of our Australian diaspora that link our two countries together."

When the sun went down, they packed up their gear and set off back along the river, to where their off-road vehicle was parked. As they approached a high-pitched whining noise grew louder and closer. Before the source of the noise was directly overhead, Ken was flattened by Chow Lim's rugby tackle, but the Wombat was not so lucky and was hit in the arm as he dived for cover behind the car. Ken's instinctive reaction was to tend to the wounded Wombat and was relieved to find he had only suffered a flesh wound, whereas a more direct hit might have severed his arm. Turning to ensure Chow Lim was OK and to thank him for saving his life, Ken was stunned to see him standing in an expert pose and pumping off long range shots at the retreating drone, from a large and lethal looking revolver. Their vehicle's cab was pierced by gaping high-calibre bullet holes but, it was still serviceable and they set off at speed to get their wounded mate to the nearest base hospital.

Melbourne, ASIO HQ

"Before you start to accuse me of duplicity Ken, I knew nothing about the true, identity of Major Chow Lim. It seems that my superiors were deliberately keeping me in the dark and using us to act as a watch on his activities."

"Well George, whoever or whatever he is I owe him my life for that rugby tackle by the river."

"I can now confirm that he is a Taiwanese intelligence agent of their National Security Bureau, sent by his government to keep tabs on the local Chinese and dissident expatriates, who favour Beijing. It seems that for some time there has been a significant leakage of Chinese government funds by corrupt officials. Much of this has been transmitted to Australia and invested in our inflated property market, drug dealing and infiltration of our strategic export industries. Now that his identity has been revealed we are being instructed from the top to cooperate with him and combine in the search for the guilty parties."

"That's a relief. It will be great to have someone on our team who understands the Chinese situation and can make sense of the difference between the parties involved."

"Meanwhile, whilst you were playing cops and bushrangers along the Murray, Kat has been making further progress in getting under the skin of the local enterprises targeted by saboteurs."

8
CHINESE WALLS

Factory for sale

"Thank you, Mrs Wu, for bringing this purchase offer to my attention. It appears on the low side despite the recent explosions and loss of production."

"The offer comes from a well-established Taiwanese food company which puts a high value on our local produce and which may want to obtain our brand name and supply contracts, with the product processing transferred to their Taipei facilities."

"It would be a blow to our economy and the loss of jobs here would damage my family's reputation, but as it stands the cost of restoring the factory to production status might prove uneconomic and our suppliers won't wait long before securing other processors. I will give it serious thought and discuss it with the board."

Melbourne, ASIO HQ

"I have been speaking with the manager of the food processing plant that was sabotaged. They have received an offer from a Taiwanese company to buy them out. That is interesting but even more significant, is the report from the merchant bankers, hired to assess its sale value.

A range of irregularities were revealed. Supplier payments did not tally with the contract prices and a growing number of mainly, Chinese, temporary workers, were paid at less than the award rate. There is no trace of the shortfall and it must be assumed that someone was raking it off the top. This together with the explosions would further depress the sale value of the business and make it more valuable to a prospective purchaser who was party to the scam."

"Who can have been responsible, Ken?"

"It could not have escaped the attention of the finance manager, Madam Wu and so the finger of suspicion points directly at her. But as she alone would not be able to raise the necessary purchase capital, we must assume she is a front for a party with deeper pockets."

"We had better consult with Major Chow Lim. He assures us that his government is not involved in trying to acquire our businesses and yet the mention of a potential Taiwanese buyer needs his explanation."

Chow Lim certainly was aware of the Taiwanese offer. He dismissed the suggestion that this was a government backed initiative, but thought it was more likely to be front men for Chinese oligarchs wanting to launder their stolen capital by purchasing a legitimate business in Australia. It would frustrate any Chinese mainland interest in acquiring the plant and its emanating from Taiwan was likely to blind-side any review by the Foreign Investments Review Board.

Invitation to tea

Kat was amongst the throng that had accepted Mrs

Wu's invitation to attend a Chinese tea party at her husband's restaurant. A range of teas was to be served with complementary Yum Cha nibbles. Those present were mainly connected with Chinese sponsored, local businesses and of these, none of the long-standing Chinese settlers were represented. Ken had suggested she get alongside the factory nursing sister and it was from her she learned that a delegation of leading Chinese oligarchs would be coming to Australia along with the Chinese Aussie Rules team, scheduled to play a return match against an Australian counterpart.

"Amongst the visiting party will be a high-ranking representative of their Foreign Affairs Department, who is either one of them or sent by the government to report on what they say and do here."

After the game

The game between the Chinese and Australian club team had been more a war of attrition than an exhibition of skill. Whilst the Australians prevailed, the Chinese made up for their lack of footballing finesse with a mastery of brute physicality and sufficient stamina that allowed most of their players to play through all four quarters. Their fitness and no-holds -barred tackling suggested that most had been selected from military ranks which also ensured their on-and-off field discipline.

No songs were sung after the game, but all were invited to the tea party catered for by Mr Wu's restaurant. As well as the players, the local movers and shakers welcomed the delegation from China. Major Chow Lim played up his aches and pains, taking the focus off his real identity and he mingled amongst the Chinese listening to their chatter. Some additional waiters had been contracted to serve up such a big banquet and amongst these Kat had managed to infiltrate employees of the local Chinese restaurants who were very willing to spy on the visitors from their motherland.

A tangled web

"Well, Kat what did you find out at the dinner?"

"As we suspected, Ken, it's a complicated story with several players and competing interests. The local Chinese are divided between those with ancestry stretching back to the gold rush days, who regard themselves as loyal Australians, and the newcomer professional class such as Mr and Mrs Wu, who have taken up significant positions in business and society, and appear to hold allegiance to interests back in China. Consequently, the locals resent these interlopers and fear they may be agents of the Chinese government."

"That tallies with our suspicions but what did your informers tell you about the visiting delegation, which came out with the football team?"

"Whilst there are government representatives in the party, who are here to keep tabs on their colleagues, most of the visitors are wealthy oligarchs who seemed most pally with the Wu faction and whose main interest is in the industries that have suffered recent setbacks. In addition, to complicate matters further, there is the suggestion of a Taiwanese interest, but my people heard no reference to this and know nothing about it."

"While you were debriefing your informants, I spoke

with Major Chow Lim to get his take on the situation and he confirmed only his own presence as evidence of Taiwanese involvement and that being restricted to a watching brief over any Chinese government interference. At the same time, he drew my attention to another interested party in that most of the Chinese football team members are special forces soldiers serving in the People's Liberation Army. Anything we might do next could easily create a major political and diplomatic firestorm. We had better catch up with George and plan our next steps very carefully."

Melbourne, ASIO HQ

George heard their report and agreed that this was a far from straight-forward challenge.

"I don't doubt the accuracy of your information and analysis but before we can adopt counter strategies we must maintain the endorsement of our Director General and that requires us to produce firmer evidence of the intentions of all the Chinese parties. In doing this you will have to ensure that your activities cannot be traced back to government."

9
FOLLOWING THE MONEY

Tea at Wu's

When the waiters had cleared the table and left the private dining room, the leadership of the Oligarch faction got down to business.

"Mrs Wu, please summarise the progress made in acquiring ownership of local enterprises and in securing our investment."

"Thank you general. We now have a controlling stake in the vineyard, the dairy and food processing plants, which were acquired cheaply, as a result of the unfortunate accidents that befell them. The previous owners were eager to sell and our proposals to restore their earning and employment capacities have the enthusiastic support of the local and state politicians. The conversion of the dairy plant to the production of higher-value baby formula products boosts export earnings and the increased access to more trusted, Australian foods, satisfies the demands of our affluent middle class for quality and safety. The replacement of the vines with a wind farm boosts the state's renewable energy and even earns government subsidies."

"Well done. But what about the sabotage that made them cheaper to acquire, has that aroused any concerns?"

"As you know there have long been triad influences here and by using their connections with bikie gangs from the Queensland Gold Coast, the destruction cannot be traced to us. A small-time local newspaper editor suggested there might be some connection between the calamities, but he was silenced and the suspicions died with him."

"That leaves the issue of Australian sensitivities about growing Chinese ownership of their rural assets. How have you managed to deal with this?"

"We have been particularly careful to use transparent and legal business structures that are completely separate from Chinese government control and local business interests have been only too willing to joint venture with us and provide Australian directors to be our public face. Local banking interests have been complicit in getting around foreign investment controls and so our financial transactions have been safely conducted and secured.

You need to appreciate that attitudes in the country are different from those in the big cities. There is strong demand for economic stimulus and people who are willing and able to work. It's an election year in Victoria and there is strong support in government for Chinese investment as a counter to the traditional reliance on US and European finance. The universities could not maintain their growth without the underpinning of fee-paying, foreign, mainly Chinese, students and the Chinese government has set up cultural bodies within them to both maintain a strong controlling influence on their students and to ensure China's culture and miraculous growth are perceived in a favourable light."

A round of applause showed the collective appreciation of the gathering at this positive report and the evening ended with toasts to the continued success of their Australian enterprises. In leaving the premises none were aware of the Chinese waiter who switched off his recorder and slipped unseen from behind a service screen.

Joining the dots

Ken turned off the recorder and congratulated Kat on eavesdropping on the oligarchs' meeting.

"Your people really came through for you with this Kat. It confirms our suspicions but more importantly it joins the missing dots between the oligarchs' strategy, their business meddling and the coordinating role played by the Wus."

George agreed but didn't comment on whether this totally explained what the Chinese were up to.

"What do you think Chow Lim?"

"It's good to know the ins and outs of the wealthy Chinese scheming and how they are seeking to secure their ill-gotten gains in Australia but there is insufficient evidence to conclude more than that."

"What they have done so far is containable by government agencies, such as the Foreign Investment Review Board and curtailing their consorting with criminals is within the jurisdiction of the Federal Police. I am beginning to suspect, George, that there is more to this than we know, and that Kat and I have been used, once more, as stalking horses to expose a far more serious threat to Australia."

"I'm afraid the answer to your suspicions is above my pay grade. But you have done what was asked of you. Thanks to you and Kat the strange goings on in Victoria and Chinese involvement, are no longer a complete mystery. The PLA 'footballers' have gone home, the closer focus on the oligarch's investment in Victorian business has stopped the vandalism and pirating of factories and farms and the key local protagonists such as madam Wu have heeded the 'gypsy's warning' for fear of losing their citizenship, if they continue to disrupt local commerce."

"As you say George, that seems to wrap things up. Thanks for the chance to work with you again and for trusting us with this assignment."

In or out of the game?

"Ken I'm in desperate need of a drink and you are invited to join me."

When the waiter had delivered their drinks, Kath drank deeply and gave full vent to her frustration?

"Did you really swallow George's answer?"

"No, it was pure bull-dust and his half-hearted dismissal was not at all like George's usual style. I cannot believe that this is all the story. Who sent the armed drone after us and why? This seems too extreme an action for the oligarchs and why were there soldiers in the football team? I sense a greater influence of the Chinese state at play here but so far it is keeping to the shadows, using the oligarchs as a distraction from their main game."

"Too right Ken. George was unusually unforthcoming,

almost shifty, and I'm sure that Choy Lim suspects more than he was prepared to say. This game has not finished, and I'm pissed-off that we have been dropped."

"You are right. There is more to play for and likewise I don't like to be left out after we have done so much and have more to contribute."

"But we have been officially signed off the case and would have no official mandate if we continued our involvement without George's blessing."

"That's it! Now I understand. Maybe we have not really been dropped. George is such a devious, bastard that the weakness of his seeming dismissal was really an unspoken invitation to keep going, off the books of course and in the event of a stuff-up, completely deniable. Thanks Kat. You helped me see the contradiction in his behaviour and I believe we still have his covert blessing. Rather than seek his permission, let's see what else we can bring to him and should we be wrong, we can at least humbly seek his forgiveness."

"I'm game, if you are, so let's decide what to do next."

"We have been told there is no evidence of Chinese intrusion into our affairs, other than that we have uncovered so far, and especially none confirming direct collusion with Beijing. If they are as complicit as we suspect, they have hidden their presence well, but there must be some way of penetrating the screen of commercial and cultural normality obscuring their less, friendly intentions. But where would you look for a loose thread?"

"We have not spotted any obvious foreign ring-leader so perhaps we should focus on pro-Chinese Australians, especially those with skin in the game. Nobody leaks information better than a politician. What about that government minister you were introduced to at the Clancy homestead party?"

"Yes, of course. Senator Baker. He offered to help me see through the false impressions I might get from the locals and ensure that my book would tell the true story of country Victoria. He was keen to attract Chinese investment and would be anxious not to frighten them off."

10
BACK IN THE GAME

Melbourne, Windsor Hotel

The minister's invitation to meet over lunch at the Windsor was very much to Ken's liking. The historic dining room and its plain but tasty fare compared more than favourably with its counterpart at Manchester's Midland. He suspected that the choice of this venue, rather than a more formal encounter in his grand ministerial office, reflected the diminished importance of their meeting in the minister's eyes and Ken was hopeful that this and his eager indulgence in a rich Victorian Shiraz would put him off his guard. Senator Baker was already seated at a table discreetly located to ensure the privacy of their meeting.

"Good afternoon Minister and thank you for inviting me to lunch at such a historic venue."

"G'day Ken, welcome to the Windsor. Yes, it's truly a Melbourne icon. But, as this is a social meeting we need not stand on ceremony and as I have presumed to use your first name, feel free to call me Tom."

"At our last meeting Tom, you offered to give me your insights into Victoria's development story."

"I am glad you followed up with me because I don't want you to be misled by bar room tales, rumour and bush prejudice towards newcomers and strangers, especially with regard to our Chinese friends who are doing so much to help turbo-charge our economic development. I am aware that there have been some minor problems with the acceptance of more recent Chinese arrivals and ill-feeling on the part of long-established settlers who resent the newcomers' success and growing influence in rural areas. But the future contribution Chinese money and know how will make is far too important to be jeopardised by such small-minded resistance."

"It's clear you feel strongly about the benefits of Chinese involvement. Could you elaborate on what their areas of contribution are and how I can get to know more about them, without treading on any sensitive toes?"

"I certainly do and as this is an election year my government's re-election will depend upon our perceived ability to deliver on major initiatives and especially those reliant on Chinese backing. It is vital that sensitivities are respected and I am pleased to hear you are attuned to this."

"What do you see as the most vital examples of beneficial Chinese contribution?"

"Broadly they fall into five areas: Education; Energy; Defence; Telecommunications and International trade. These areas are vital for broadening our economic growth and reducing our total reliance on commodity exports. You must understand that these prospects are not just a Victorian state issue but even more importantly, critical to our national prosperity, growth and security."

"You sum it up much more succinctly than anyone else I have spoken to but how do I learn more without upsetting the apple cart and who are the inside movers and shakers I should meet and speak with?"

In response the Senator spoke at length but had lapsed into familiar 'pollie' speech which said a lot but meant nothing of substance. Ken could see he would get nothing of further value from him but left pleased that he had at least confirmed areas of prospective Chinese interference and with savoury taste-bud memories of the Windsor's prime rib of beef.

The Grand, Richmond

Kat savoured her refreshing lemon lime and bitters as Ken reported on his lunch with Senator Baker.

"Can't say I am surprised by the trademark political brush-off but as you say Ken, his five areas of key interaction between Australian and Chinese interests confirms the target areas that need deeper exploration. What we have detected so far is just the river's surface but the hidden undercurrents are the driving force we need to expose."

"You are right Kat and the key to finding out more is to seek out the key players and uncover their strategies and organisations. We will not find them in the bush but there must be insiders, loyal to Australia, who could give us some leads. I think I know just the person to set us on the right path."

11
PLUMBING THE DEPTHS

Chez Cochin

The reputation of a noted Franco-Vietnamese restaurant in Richmond and the added lure of Kat's company, were more than enough to ensure Jack accepted Ken's invitation to dine with them.

"Thanks for inviting me here. I know I should focus on the Vietnamese, specialties but this chateaubriand is to die for. It's good of you to expand my Melbourne culinary experience but I suspect you have more self-interested motives and will expect me to sing for my supper."

"Spot on Jack. But as you set us off on this course of action, you too have skin in the game. Senator Baker highlighted the key areas of Chinese interest but was not forthcoming about who the movers and shakers might be. ASIO has been equally unforthcoming, despite our work in your back yard, but it occurred to us that there must be insiders, perhaps even potential whistle blowers worth contacting, and who better than an astute and well informed journalist to introduce us to the right people."

"You are right Ken, but I must caution you that there is a strong protective pro-Chinese lobby of academics, business people, deeply indebted to Chinese partners, serving and former politicians and even mainstream journalists of a left leaning persuasion. Any questioning and critical analysis of Chinese doings in Australia meets with fierce push-back from this protective shield and some parts of the deeply entrenched Chines diaspora. This reaction, whilst mostly employing public ridicule and accusations of racism, can even extend to violent acts of retribution as you have already experienced up along the Murray. So, in agreeing to reveal a useful contact I am concerned to ensure both yours and their safety."

"We are highly attuned to the pitfalls involved in speaking truth to power but Ken and I bear the personal scars of thwarting the malign acts of ruthless state sponsored terrorists who are all too happy to hide behind our liberal western legal protections. We could not have succeeded without the support of brave people prepared to take the risk of informing against these dark forces."

"Thank you for that Kat. Your reputation and record convince me that you are to be trusted to do your utmost to protect any source I reveal to you and to make the most of what they can tell you to protect Australia's interests."

Bell, book and by-line

"What do you think of Jack's suggestion of talking with a newshound?"

"It depends very much who and what sort of journalist he is putting forward. Painstaking, well-researched and impartial analysis of information is being replaced by the unquestioned click-bait of the twenty-four-hour news cycle. Many of the older experienced journos are being sacked or retired and replaced by cheaper, compliant scribes from university journalism schools, strongly opinionated but lacking experience on the job and of life in general."

"Too true Kat and these are the prolific and growing purveyors of false news. At least the meeting place Jack proposes is the more likely lair of real news hounds of the old school rather than the inner-city latte lounges and smashed avocado hang-outs surrounding our national broadcaster's HQ."

It was in the brasserie of Young and Jackson's that they found Dennis who was taking a lunch break from his office across Swanston Street where he worked at St Paul's Cathedral, as a PR adviser to the Anglican Archbishop of Melbourne and occasional correspondent for the *Church Times* in London. Despite being past the biblical ordained life span, Dennis leaped to his feet, shook Ken's hand, embraced Kat and asked them what they would like to drink. Kat and Ken were so surprised by the identity of Jack's recommended source they needed a drink and a very stiff one when he urged them to drop the "Father" tag and call him just Den. He was both a journalist and as his clerical collar confirmed, a priest to boot.

"It's clear from the look on your faces that I am not what you expected and you are wondering how a priest and small-time journalist can give you what you are looking for."

"You have it in one Den. Kat and I were expecting a hard-drinking, heavy smoking, life-scarred, newsman, either retired or on the way out."

"I like a dram, don't smoke, and no longer practise as a priest. I am a Church Times Australian correspondent but in recognition of my past journalistic eminence I still contribute the occasional column to national and international papers and magazines on dealing with China and I speak and read Mandarin fluently. So, does that alleviate some of your misconceptions?"

"Yes, it does but when I have got us another round of drinks perhaps you will flesh out your story a bit more."

"Before I do that, you need to know that Jack has told me all about your backgrounds and your mission. But, don't be alarmed. As I will explain, in the past I too have been subject to the Official Secrets Act and so all that is said here will stay in confidence and not even Jack will know what we have discussed. Getting to the guts of how and why my background is relevant to your interests: as a young and naïve, newly ordained Anglican priest from Selwyn College Cambridge, I followed in Bishop Selwyn's footsteps by becoming a curate in a Hong Kong parish from which I graduated into missionary work in Communist China and became steeped in Chinese culture, language and politics.

"That explains your China exposure but where does the official secrets act come into this and your relevant journalistic experience.?"

"At first I was a truly devout and dedicated missionary with some considerable sympathy with what the Chinese government was trying to do for its people. But all of that changed with the wickedness of Mao's Cultural Revolution and the excesses of the Red Guard. Many of my Chinese Christian friends and colleagues were imprisoned tortured and even executed. I was detained, survived some months of hard labour in a timber harvesting Gulag near the Soviet border and was fortunate only to be deported back to Hong Kong. It was this experience that forged my love of Chinese people and culture and sowed the seeds of my undying mistrust and hatred of their political system and its masters.

This made me ripe for recruitment by MI6 who trained me as an agent and infiltrated me back into the mainland on several missions, especially during the turbulent years of succession after Mao's death and during the Tiananmen Square crisis, leading up to the massacre. Latterly, when the preparations for the handover of Hong Kong to Chinese sovereignty made for a relaxing of tensions between Britain and the Communist rulers, I travelled in the guise of an international correspondent for the South China Morning Post and when MI6 began to rely more on electronic surveillance via the five eyes alliance I stopped being a full-time agent and intensified my journalistic work as a 'China expert', contracting to a wide range of English speaking media, including British and American TV companies. This kept me occupied, closely in touch with Chinese affairs through contacts even in high level government positions and honed my journalistic skills, until the more recent change of leadership and intense internal surveillance and control of Chinese citizens, which exposed my missionary past and made me persona non grata in China until the present day.

My current role is a sort of retirement reward for my past service to the church, aided and abetted by my former secret service employers who consult with me as needed and I still maintain my network of significant contacts in China and amongst the diaspora here in Australia, which keeps me up to date with Chinese activities and their covert strategic motivation."

Ken and Kat were left completely in awe of Den's story and the hard-won expertise he had accumulated. He was clearly the key to accessing the influencers and leaders directing Chinese interference and disruption of Australian affairs. The question was how could contact be made with them without arousing Chinese suspicions and stirring up the pro-Chinese, Australian sympathisers?

Den cautioned against tarring all Chinese with the same brush. He pointed to three groupings:

"First are the long-established ancestors of 19th century gold prospectors who, although feeling some pride at the rise of a more powerful and influential China on the world stage, are completely assimilated into their new homeland and loyal to Australia. Some, as you have discovered have personal reasons for extreme mistrust and hatred of the communist regime. This group can provide you with collaborators and informants who are more suited to infiltrating the ethic groupings you are targeting.

The more recent wave of immigrants is mostly focused on the opportunities offered in the more open and prosperous Australian society, to build better lives for themselves and secure futures for their children. These aspirations are laudable and pose no risk except that amongst them are those former state apparatchiks who have transferred wealth that arguably was stolen from the state and invested it here in property and Australian business enterprises. Those behind the sabotage and disruption you have uncovered, especially represented by the likes of Madam Wu, are obvious examples of this type. Whilst their motivation is primarily personal greed, they are vulnerable to Chinese government blackmail, especially those with family members still living in China and their children represent a useful fifth column in our universities and strategic industries. At the very least you will need to guard your backs against a possible threat from this source.

That brings me to those who you need to focus on most and beware of at risk of your lives. These are committed Chinese agents, some of them sleepers, hidden and lying dormant for years amongst the more benign Chinese community, who have been woken and tasked with stealing business secrets, technological know-how and damaging Australia in a variety of ways. They are embedded in the sectors I have already identified, and these must be the targets of your explorations.

Above all, I implore you, do not let the evils you will uncover blind you to the essential character and virtues of the Chinese people. The guilty party is the Chinese Communist Party which drives and controls all aspects of Chinese life and external relations by suppressing their people and imposing a false dogma."

Having thanked Den for the advice and identities he had given them, Kat and Ken agreed secure means of keeping in touch with him and left to plan a course of action.

12

HARVESTING HEARTS AND MINDS

Confucius says

Kat and Ken walked up Swanston Street and turned into Flinders Lane, with much to think about after their meeting with Den. Suddenly, Ken suggested they stop for some food to soak up their drinks and led her into Centre Way, heading back down to De Graves Street. Increasing his pace, Ken tripped down the stairs into Centre Place and nudged Kat into one of its cave-like, micro cafés. Barely had she taken a seat and caught her breath when Ken pulled her into his embrace and kissed her with passionate abandon. Whilst she didn't resist him, she was not wholehearted in reciprocating his ardour and when he released her, she shaped up to ask him what he was playing at.

"Has he gone past?" Ken asked and turned to look both ways along the lane looking for any trace of the follower who had been dogging their steps since they had left the pub. Kat caught on quickly and confirmed that she had not seen anyone following them. They decided to wait a little longer before resuming their walk to be sure they had shaken off their tail and were waiting for their coffees when they felt someone slip on to the end of their bench and ask, politely,

"Is there room for one more spy on this seat?"

"Chow Lim, you rascal what are you doing following us?"

Suppressing his superior smirk at having exposed their poor trade craft, he apologised for sneaking up on them and assured them that he was the only party on their trail.

"I suspected that you would not take George's brush-off too literally and that you were more likely than me to succeed, undetected, in smoking out the guilty parties. How did you go with Den? Did he give you any promising leads?"

Ken confirmed the focus of their next enquiries but whilst he trusted Chow Lim, he withheld any names until he and Kat had checked them out.

"The university is probably the best place to start and we will be trying to learn more about who's who in the Confucius Institute."

"That's a good idea. The organisation promotes Chinese culture and is funded by the Communist Government, which demands strict control over what is taught by its academics. When you have narrowed your enquiries let me know and I will be able to provide you with some inside information."

Chow Lim would not be drawn further on this offer and having declined a coffee said he had to be away, slipped out of the café and disappeared into the passing crowd.

The Chinese century

The Dean of the Asian Studies department and chairman of the Confucius Institute was pleased to meet with an author writing about both past and contemporary developments in Victoria and invited Ken to come to his office for tea and a chat. Professor Li Wei looked far from Ken's preconception of what an orientalist should be. He wore a sharp pin-striped suit and his black brogues reflected a mirror shine. He was well groomed and looked more like an American executive than a Chinese academic. His trans-Atlantic accent supported this initial impression although, it was more the product of early education at an American missionary school and post-graduate studies in America. He smiled a great deal and his welcoming greeting further supported the image of a confident, self-made man.

"I am so glad that you have approached the horse's mouth, so to speak, rather than relying on those journalists and politicians of an anti-Chinese persuasion, to inform you about our work here."

"I am delighted Professor that you are willing to talk with me and I am keen to understand the role that Chinese culture and thought are playing in Australia today."

"Firstly, and most importantly you must understand the independence of our approach. Whilst we receive funding from both Australian and Chinese government sources, the Institute is focused on offering cultural and language programs for our local communities under the direction of a senior university academic. We do not engage in management of any award courses of the university nor in other academic endeavours of the university and so there is no impact on academic autonomy and independence".

"So, could you elaborate further on the focus and content of your teaching?"

"As a writer, you will be aware of the rise of China over recent years and as a result of the strong trade interdependence between our countries and the growing presence of Chinese students at the university, it is imperative that a true picture of China's long history and culture is painted as a context in which this has occurred. At the same time, we recognise the involvement of early Chinese settlers who came to discover gold and stayed to develop the outback and whose offspring are now contributing greatly to Australian business and the professions."

For the next hour the professor waxed eloquent about the new economic rise of China and why this needs to be respected because of the good it has done to increase the prosperity of its people and those of the countries which are partners in Chairman Xi's Belt and Road initiative. He was sufficiently subtle to avoid any impression of hubris and stayed very, clear of the more contentious issues of its military adventurism in the South China Sea, suppression of the Uighurs, its treatment of Hong Kong and harassment of Taiwan.

Ken was impressed by the Professor's diplomatic demeanour but came away wanting to find out what really happened inside the Confucius Institute classrooms. It was time to take Chow Lim up on his offer of help.

Another Chinese face

The small group of young Chinese men and women finished the meal that Kat and Ken had treated them to and Chow Lim welcomed them and thanked them for agreeing to help. He had explained that, not all of the Chinese students at the university came from the mainland. Some from Hong were less wedded to their new government and a few others were Taiwanese, of which a select group were agents of Taiwan's National Security Bureau and trusted operatives controlled by Major Chow Lim.

Ken explained what he and Kat were looking for and gave them a summary of what the Professor had told him. They smiled sardonically at the story of China's century and were eager to counter with their experience of what actually happened in these classes. A bright young woman challenged the purported purpose of the Institute.

"Despite what he said, the Institute is tightly controlled by a board which is dominated by Chinese government representatives, loyal members of the community in Victoria and useful idiots from Australian society whose eyes are blinded to all but the good that the growingly influential Chinese government is doing for Australia and their personal wellbeing. Its real purpose is to spread false propaganda about China's strategy, influence and control of both Chinese students and key members of the resident Chinese, who hold down influential positions in business, professions, state and local politics."

"But how do they get away with this under the noses of the university's leadership?"

"They are so focused on keeping and growing the financial stake that comes with establishment of the Institute and Chinese students, that they have failed to sign any controlling agreement and turn a blind eye to the dominant influence of the Chinese government."

"But, what about the students, do they just accept this placidly?"

A tall, intelligent looking young man laughed derisorily at this and took up the story.

"Only recently has there been some push back because of the unrest in Hong Kong and news of the genocidal imprisoning of Uighurs in hidden gulags. There has been at least one protest on the campus, but this was challenged by pro-Beijing students and a somewhat disengaged and complicit media gave it little coverage. As for the Professor-there is much more than meets the eye when you encounter him and risk falling under the spell of his charm."

Another student, unlike the others, was born and bred in Australia and worked for a local bank. His contribution painted a much more sinister picture of the professor's power and influence.

"Over recent years, Chinese sleeper agents have been activated and use their respected positions in the local Chinese community to further the interests of their Beijing masters. They have infiltrated local government councils by bribery and manipulation of party 'warlords' and some are on the brink of breaking into the Federal Parliament. They use their positions to ferment opposition to Australian government policies seen as counter to Chinese influence and appoint former ministers, academics and fellow traveller journalists to lucrative positions on the boards of Chinese enterprises and in Chinese-Australian friendship societies. These are very, dangerous trends and their tentacles are spreading rapidly. It is not widely known that this network is managed and controlled by the good professor Li Wei. We suspect that he is really a senior agent in the Chinese secret service and that his seditious contacts spread far beyond the university. He is dangerous to cross and it is suspected that his hounding of the young man from country Victoria, who committed suicide, forced him to take his own life."

Kat and Ken had struck gold but how could they capitalise on this information and how could they gather evidence beyond the testimony of these courageous young people. They were soon to find out.

13
MAN ON THE RUN

Ken was catapulted from the warm depths of a delightful dream by the insistent ringing of his mobile phone. A quick glance at the screen showed it was the ungodly hour of three in the morning, but the identity of the caller was unclear.

"Hi Ken. Sorry to wake you so early. Its Chow Lim. We have a problem. You recall the bright young local who revealed so much about Chinese political disruption. He left an alarm call on my answering service and now he is missing. Let's meet and see what we can do to find him, if it's not too late."

Kat and Kim met Chow Lim in the all-night Greek restaurant on Lonsdale Street. They had barely begun to talk when Kat's phone rang. She listened with a very, concerned look on her face.

"Thank you for letting us know. He is in great danger and you must hide him until we can get there and take him to somewhere safe." Kat then advised the caller to close the call.

"That was the wife of the Chinese restaurant owner whose son committed suicide. It seems your agent was a mate of her late son and last night he turned up on their doorstep. He was in a bit of a bad way-showing signs of some rough handling and scared out of his wits."

Chow Lim went outside to make a call for assistance and Ken decided it was time to call on Pete and his former SAS mates to provide much needed back up.

The Military helicopter carrying Ken, Kat, Chow Lim, Pete and six of his squaddies, raced over Bendigo on its way north. The endangering of Chow Lim's agent had influenced George more than Ken could have achieved in calling on the RAAF to provide this urgent mercy flight. It was decided to keep police out of it at this stage and Jack had been called on to provide a minibus to take them to the suburban restaurant.

Johnny Chow was badly knocked about and even more nervously distraught. Two bikies had set on him and managed to get in a few blows and kicks before he was able to pull a knife and cut them up so badly, they had to let him go. A discreet and collaborative Chinese doctor had been called and after patching up the wounds he gave Johnny a sedative to calm him and put him to sleep.

Chow Lim's primary concern was for his agent and whilst it would have been easy to whisk him away, with secret service help, a council of war decided that here was an opportunity to hit back at the opposition and learn more about the extent of their operations and players. It was certain that Johnny would be pursued, and it was Kat who came up with the idea of calling on Wombat for some help in setting up an ambush. After his being shot during their last encounter with Chinese agents and their attempt to hunt him down, he was more than willing to seize a chance for revenge.

Back to the Victorian Bush

Allowing rumours to leak into the local Chinese community that a wounded student had fled from Melbourne and was hiding in the bush along the Murray river, had proved effective in luring his attackers into the open. A hit squad was reported to be asking questions around the area and despite attempts to lead them astray, they had been sighted along the river and were deploying drones to search for their quarry.

Ken, Kat, Pete, and his SAS mates were a step ahead of them and were based in one of the Wombat's hideouts, securely concealed by the surrounding bush. A false trail had been laid to draw the pursuers on and each member of the team was in place, ready to close the trap. The haunting cry of a Boobook owl shattered the nocturnal silence of the bush, signalling that their prey was nearby.

The Chinese party's officer was the first to detect smoke seeping in from the surrounding bush.

"Where is that smoke coming from sergeant?"

"I don't know sir, perhaps it is from a campfire. It means they are very, close."

"That's more than campfire smoke. I have heard of how dangerous bushfires can be and how quickly they can spread and trap the unwary. Quickly, call in your men and have them fall back away from where the smoke is coming from."

Then as the sergeant opened his radio to call the men, a curtain of fire arose where the smoke had been and moved rapidly to encircle their position.

"We are in danger of being surrounded sir what should we do?"

"Quick man, head for the river. That's the only way we can escape."

Pete's men were not as accomplished as the Wombat in imitating owl, calls but they did their best to signal as the Chinese raced towards the riverbank and plunged into the swiftly flowing waters. Their successful rout alerted the team of locals to stop the cool burn they had started and allow the fire to peter out as it encroached on a well, placed fire break.

"Great job you guys and thanks Wombat. You really sent them packing."

"A pleasure Ken. That river is full of fast-moving water coming down from storms in the top end. Its currents are treacherous and below the surface it is very cold. Some of those guys will not make it back and any that do will certainly think twice about taking us on in the bush again."

"Too right and as we anticipated this possible line of retreat, those who manage to swim to safety will be intercepted by the armed police, manning fast launches just downstream of us."

"What happened to their drone that was tracking us?"

"Pete's guys took care of that with some kit they brought along which sent it wildly off course and crashing into the trees."

The fire roasted duck and yabbies, back at Wombat's camp, were more than welcome and when they had eaten their fill, Kat and Ken listened eagerly as the fugitive Chinese student told his tale.

"Li Wei used his position with the Confucius Institute to both promote Chinese culture and more importantly, to use influential Australians and Chinese sleeper agents to subvert Australian economic and political institutions. Native Australians were appointed to the boards of Chinese owned companies and programmed to defend Chinese government activities. Bribery and various forms of patronage were used to influence political processes such as branch stacking and putting up favoured candidates for party and government offices.

The Belt and Road initiative appears economically appealing and the Victorian State government has been seduced into considering cooperation to boost the state's economic progress. The Federal government is well, aware of the crippling debt burdens placed on other countries who bought in and how the ownership of key assets such as strategic ports have become significant military staging posts for the Chinese navy and commercial fleets. Consequently, they have stood back from joining this initiative and have tightened scrutiny of Chinese investments and business interventions, especially in such areas as telecommunications and agriculture. Wi Lei has made significant use of this tool to enhance Chinese influence and power in Australia."

"While you have been recovering from your injuries my colleague, Kat, has checked on Wi Lei's movements and it seems he has gone back to China and is unlikely to return. Will that disrupt and eventually destroy this insidious enterprise?"

"By no means. Whilst he has been a significant player, he was only one member of a leadership network whose web of influence reaches into strategic scientific research and defence industries. You must not stop now and further enquiries need to be focused on defence programs, such as submarine development, contractors to the F35 Stealth Fighter and the building of the Hunter Class Frigates. Another area of concern for you is the seemingly innocuous collaborative work being undertaken in your universities on Biotechnology and Artificial Intelligence, between your best scientists and Chinese counterparts.

The fact that more has not been done already to investigate this infiltration is both due to Australian overconfidence in its security services and the extent to which the Chinese have made this a no go area because of your economic dependence on Chinese trade and investment. It is good that you have come on the scene, before it is too late, and I thank you very much for saving my life."

"Thank you, Johnny for your courage in exposing this threat to our security. You will be safe here in Wombat's care until Major Lim arranges for your return to your home in Taiwan."

14
DEFENCE OF THE REALM

The science of defence

"The key challenge facing defence science is to prevail in a hostile, competitive, environment. Our work is focused on developing the abilities to do this and whilst we rely on cooperation with our five eyes partners, we must ensure that we can meet and overcome the potential threats in our zones of strategic interest. Consequently, we are concentrating on command and control in the air, on and under the sea and in both stellar and cyber space. In doing this we are working in collaboration with private enterprise and our leading research universities. The ability to call on the abilities of these parties, especially the growing local defence industries is a great strength but, in sharing knowledge and information with them exposes vulnerabilities posed by infiltration and disruption by hostile interests. As my remit is principally scientific, I will continue to describe some of our initiatives and trust ASIS to secure and protect our work against espionage."

"The Chief Defence Scientist was very impressive in her painting of the bigger picture and she left me in no doubt of the need to defend theft and disruption of the real capabilities we have and are developing."

"That's why I called you and Kat in to meet her. Now you understand the scope of our challenge, it is the secret services task to identify the enemy parties and negate their incursions and I want you to continue working for us to pull this off."

"But surely, with all your resources George you can't expect us to succeed where you can't."

"No Kat, you are only partially right. We are aware of the areas of threat and can call up powerful resources when needed but our problem is targeting the hidden, key disruptors who are pulling the strings. We are hamstrung by the seeming love-hate relationship between us and China and the protective shield they have deployed, manned by Australian fellow travellers and self-interested defenders. If we go in all guns blazing, without explicit political support and unquestionable evidence of malfeasance, we would soon be muzzled and called off. On the other hand, as you have already ably demonstrated, you can slip under their radar and spot the targets for us to destroy. Also, remember you are not entirely alone as you have the fully authorised support of Major Chow Lim, the Reverend Dennis and your underground army of ex-SAS men and the Wombat.

I am sorry to have brushed you off before but thankfully, as expected, you saw through my subterfuge and persevered. I hope you will not hold that against me and agree to continue to contribute to this vital work."

"Ken and I are fully committed to the national cause and we are determined to continue to search out and frustrate these renegades and undercover agents. We are not completely unknown to Chinese agents as a result of our clash in the bush and in order to go further we will need to place some assets inside the organisations that they are working to undermine."

"Thank you. Just keep me posted using our existing secure communications procedure and now I have arranged for you to be transported, incognito, back to Melbourne."

Perth, Under the sea

The Australian advanced submarine project and frigate build were divided between ship building facilities in Adelaide and Perth. The main media focus was on these locations and a continual questioning of the chosen vessels' suitability, availability and the reliability and security of the foreign contract winners. One of the many obstacles that threatened to delay the work was the unavailability of skilled, shipyard workers and so, it had not been too difficult to infiltrate Pete and some of his men into the Western Australian yard. Components were manufactured and assembled in both states and it was common for these parts to be transported between the respective yards, as needed, and others came in from and were exchanged with sub-contractors at other locations.

Ken returned from the bar with schooners of beer and delivered them to a table in a secluded part of the Subiaco pub.

"Cheers Pete. Good to see you again. How are you finding life in WA?"

"Bit quiet compared with back east but some parts of Perth are lively enough. Not that the pressures of shift work at the yard allow for too many regular leisure breaks."

"Anything of interest to report?"

"At first I wondered why you got me transferred to this sleepy hollow, away from the main action in Adelaide but whilst there is not much sign of irregularities here other than the usual pilfering of tools and scrap materials for the building of hobby farm projects, I have noted an increase in the transfer out of some specialist steel components to the Stirling naval base on Garden island. What's peculiar about them, is that they are designed to withstand deep, under sea, pressures and yet Stirling has no involvement in the submarine program."

"Perhaps they are of a secret nature and from Stirling they are being shipped to Adelaide?"

"That's where this gets interesting. One of my blokes managed to get himself assigned to the delivery crew in case any component needed damage repair in transit. He's a very cheery type and by shouting some of the matelots in their wet canteen they were sufficiently indiscreet to tell him that the components were not shipped on to the East, nor did they stay at the base. That's all they knew, and it took all of his romantic whiles to find out from a female logistics officer, that some otherwise unidentified cargoes were heading north along the WA coast. But to what destination she did not know."

George was unable to identify a naval base in that part of the world where the major port facilities were dedicated to the export of minerals and gas. But he was able to provide Ken with a tracking device that Pete could attach to the next shipment due to go north. A few weeks later all was revealed when a navy ship from Stirling was tracked as far north as Karratha, where it stopped in the port of Dampier for a while before returning south. But ken and Kat were no wiser as there was no known navy facility in that locality.

In the Pirate's lair

Karratha was a great surprise to Kat and Ken. It had grown and flourished due to its minerals and gas export facilities and the workforce it drew in. But unlike other Pilbara towns reliant on mining, it had made a special effort to encourage an otherwise fly in fly out workforce, to bring their families and settle, despite its harsh climate. The central cluster of attractive, modern buildings and pavement cafés reflected its prosperity and growing liveability. There were several lively watering holes that attracted cashed up workers from the LNG plant on the nearby Burrup Peninsula and especially suited to their purpose, those offering sports coverage, gambling facilities and hearty bar meals

The courtesy bus dropped them at the Tav Sports bar just as the lively evening session was kicking off. Aussie rules matches, rugby league games and horse racing, dominated the panoramic TV screens and the noise of the seething mass of patrons was deafening. Although most of the clientele was local and male it was not unusual for round-Australia tourists to drop in for dinner and Kat and Kim were dressed for the part and caused no untoward comment.

They were careful to slowly infiltrate themselves into the crowd and only after enjoying super-sized seafood dinners, did they start to engage with a group of men and women sitting apart from the noisier throng.

"So, you're up from the south to enjoy our winter sun?"

"Yes, we come from Victoria and I'm introducing my friend Ken to the real Australia. My name's Kat by the way."

After a following round of handshakes and introductions they were thoroughly grilled about their backgrounds and interests and their shouting of drinks soon won them the friendly acceptance of the easy-going crowd.

"We are very impressed by the new Karratha and guess it must be a good place to live."

"Yea it's much better than living in a bachelor work camp and the money makes up for the hard summers and occasional cyclones and as my wife will confirm it's been great to keep the family together and the kids thrive in the outdoor life."

"Do you get out and about much when you're not working?"

"Sure do. We fish a lot up and down the coast and we have the best of boats and gear that we just couldn't afford on the wages down south."

"One thing puzzled us. The ores and energy you export are pretty vital to our economy, but we don't see any defence force presence to protect you from attacks by terrorists or the like."

"I guess we are too remote for anything like that to happen without early warning and we have coast watch planes keeping an eye out for illegal immigrants and further north, the radar covers miles of the sea approaches. Also, there are Norforce units that patrol the outback and call in anything unusual going on. But there are no dedicated naval facilities here."

"That's reassuring. We would like to see more of the coastline before we move on and how would you suggest we do that?"

"Hey Clarry! Come over here and meet some wise people from the east who could use your tour guide services."

The tall dark-skinned man called Clarry peeled himself off from his gang of mates and came across to meet Kat and Ken.

"G'day! I show small groups around for a price-but it's not too dear depending on where you want to go and for how long. As you can see, I am a local. I'm born and bred in these parts and being aboriginal enables me to gain access to tribal lands where the best rock art can be seen."

"That sounds great. We understand the Burrup Peninsula is worth a visit, despite the gas plant and we anticipate a day or overnight trip."

"That's fine. If you can be ready to start tomorrow, I will collect you from your camp site around eight o'clock."

"Great. We look forward to it and thanks to you all for your company and setting this up for us."

Clarry proved to be an excellent guide and as well as explaining the background to the industrial development, which was very much in evidence, he entertained them with the exploits of the seventeenth century English explorer, navigator and former pirate, Dampier, who was based in this area and took them to see the statue of the red dog, hero of Louis de Bernières' book and the film. But the highlight of his tour was the Peninsula's aboriginal heritage. Stopping to brew a billy of tea, they took the opportunity to follow up on their enquiries about defence of the area.

"No, there have never been any navy facilities around here and all the land is Aboriginal owned, apart from a national park on Dolphin island to the north of the Peninsula, which is state government controlled. It's never been of much interest to my people especially as we believe it's haunted by sea spirits."

"Surely that's an ancient legend which can't be true today."

"No Kat, only recently there have been reports of lights out there in the night and on one occasion a huge shadow passed under one of our fishing boats and it was too big and deep to be a ray or dugong. Now we give that island a wide berth."

"That's interesting Clarry we'll be sure to stay away."

"That's easy. Access has been denied while the parks people rejuvenate the landscape."

Back in Karratha, ken and Kat gathered more information about the island. The parks department confirmed it was off limits due to restoration work and details of its topography suggested it was too small to host any major facilities. It was in conversation with a marine pilot that they made an interesting discovery.

"I suppose you have seen those big gas tankers moored off your Dampier campsite which are waiting to take on LNG for export."

"Yes, and the lights and flares from the plant on the peninsula light up the sky at night."

"But that's not all the facilities out there. You can't see it from the shore, but there is a massive floating gas processing vessel moored out there. As a result of environmental dithering by the state government about establishing a plant near Broome, she was brought up to boost the onshore capacity and as an insurance against the environmental activists restricting or even shutting down the peninsula plant. Its supplies come up from Perth and nobody is allowed out there other than its crew, all of which are flown in and helicoptered out to it."

Despite this promising lead, further enquiries about the vessel soon ran dry. They could find no reference to an ownership company and it appeared to operate completely independently of any offshore support and supplies. But their trawl for information unearthed a small research group which was on attachment from a South Australian university. Kat had met up with one of their scientists in a Karratha hair dressing salon and they got on so well this chance contact led to lunch.

"You are marine researchers exploring the possibilities for developing fishing industries along the north west coast?"

"If we are successful you may one day be enjoying succulent oysters from these parts."

Kat ordered two more glasses of the crisp cool chardonnay to accompany their grilled lobsters and noted its common South Australian origin with those of the researchers.

"You seem to be far from your natural base and what

do your Western Australian colleagues think of you rooting around in their back yard?"

"That's no problem as we won an open competition for the work and as you know the finest oysters come from our Coffin Bay. In fact, we are somewhat of a cross-cultural group with a few yanks amongst us and even a senior scientist of Chinese origin."

Kat was quick to share this information with Ken and they agreed that whilst the research story was plausible, they wondered whether marine research capability from South Australia merited bringing to work in the west.

"If it had been won by open competition it's hard to believe they would have outgunned rivals from the like of Queensland's pre-eminent James Cook University and what about CSIRO input?"

"Exactly my thoughts too, Ken and what's more, when I told her that my family had some oyster farm interests in Southern NSW, she was anxious to change the subject and focus more on Ningaloo Reef and other wonders of the north west."

"Then there was the reference to a scientist of Chinese origin. Maybe a coincidence but one I think worth following up."

They were further intrigued to hear confirmation from George's discreet enquiries that indeed the researchers did come from a South Australian university. But one that, rather than specialising in fisheries research, was working closely with Defence Science on shipbuilding technology associated with Australia's advance submarine and frigate programs. Furthermore, the informative scientist is an eminent professor of robotics, specialising in the digital planning and construction of a whole ship. The Chinese scientist, who is an Australian citizen, was on a short-term assignment in WA and was usually based in the Osborne shipbuilding yard in Adelaide where his expertise is focused on artificial intelligence applications to maritime warfare.

It was time to find out what was going on off the coast of Dampier and this was best addressed by getting one of Pete's men, with specialist welding skills, posted to the naval crew that was clearly delivering components from Stirling to the so-called gas processing ship. In the meanwhile, Kat and Ken flew back to find out more about the possible Chinese 'cuckoo' in the Navy's Osborne nest.

Chuck Brown had trained as a highly specialised welder, after leaving the service, working on the most exacting pipeline jobs from the Middle East to Alaska. He had made good contacts with serving SAS troopers at Swanbourne barracks in Perth and was easily accepted as a fellow serviceman by the navy boys at Stirling. He had succeeded in hiding a hairline crack in one of the components shipped up to Dampier and when it was detected, during assembly, it was quicker and cheaper to fly him up to fix it rather than ship the cracked member all the way back.

15
PHANTOMS OF THE DEEP

Unmanned and deadly

Chuck was awe struck by the size of the gas plant vessel as his helicopter descended onto the landing zone. It was way bigger than even the largest American aircraft carriers and on approach he was intrigued to see the huge sea-level doors at its stern.

His work on the faulty component was very closely supervised and the ship's captain, a high-ranking navy officer, had reminded him of the penalties for breaching his obligations under the Official Secrets Act. Whether or not this vessel was intended primarily as a floating gas plant it was soon clear that much of it was dedicated to the assembly and launch-testing of enormous sub-surface vessels.

The engineers he worked alongside were either navy or otherwise government employed specialists who communicated the bare minimum he needed to know in carrying out his repair job. But later in their wardroom he was readily accepted as a fellow serviceman, under the same constraints imposed by secrets legislation and, within limits, they responded to his natural curiosity about their work.

"Is it true that we are bolstering the expansion of our submarine fleet with crewless underwater drones?"

"That's right Chuck. Much has been made of the risk of our depending on a building program that will only produce the bulk of our requirement by 2030, its spiralling cost and unproven capability. But our masters are not as dumb as some of the detractors and media make out."

"This is an insurance policy against the failure of the French contract?"

"Not exactly, although you could conclude that. It is really designed to complement the Barracuda sub project and still maintain our close relationship with the US Navy."

"Isn't that unnecessary and costly duplication?

"No, it's not in that it is driven by the fast, changing nature of undersea defence and the need to keep up with if not ahead of the game. The Russians are well advanced in this field and the Americans are already trialling a vessel known as Orca after the killer whale species. What's different about these boats, compared with conventional submarines is that they are unmanned, powered by new propulsion systems and can remain on station months longer than manned subs can."

"But what do they do? Are they just an unmanned version of regular subs?"

"Most importantly they will operate in conjunction with a mothership sub. Their ability to remain on station much longer, undetected, enables them to be the eyes and ears of the sub fleet and call them in when hostiles threaten our interests. This same inter-operativity will apply to their communication links with our new fighter aircraft and in a sense, they are not unlike the Wedgetail and Poseidon command and control aircraft, in action over the Middle East and defending our coast lines. Further development is giving them teeth in the shape of torpedo and missile firing capability and their lower cost will enable them to be deployed in larger numbers than conventional subs."

"What about the propulsion system. We are barred from using nuclear power?"

"That is top-secret, but you should not assume that nuclear power will always be embargoed. Growing threats in our seas of interest to our north, are becoming increasingly nuclear powered and it may not be a coincidence that our French designed diesel powered sub is really a revision of their Barracuda nuclear driven vessel, which might be susceptible to retro-conversion in future if required and approved."

"So, this ship is a test bed for a prototype unmanned boat?"

"That's right."

"Gee wouldn't the Chinese like to get their hands on this technology?"

"That's why we are testing it up here away from our usual naval facilities and shipyards and in waters close to those in which it is most likely to operate. Spying attempts are easier to detect up here and we keep a tight watch on potential foreign probes. Our real vulnerability is in the research and development centres — our collaborative universities who have sold their souls for Chinese student gold and academic interchange."

Strikeback

One of Ken's favourite indulgences on a warm summer night, in Adelaide, was the famous pie floater, served by street food cars. The meat pie floating in a bowl of glutinous pea soup, reminded him of the traditional fare of Manchester's fairground food stalls and especially the unbeatable black puddings at Bury market. Wending his way through the quiet and darkened streets on the way back to his lodging, he both digested his supper and ruminated on the meaning of Chuck's story about the secret underwater drone research. He was so engrossed in this that he neglected standard security practice and especially the approaching bicycle, without lights.

Had the bike been better maintained, its creaking chain would not have alerted him to the approaching danger and when the rider fired his silenced pistol, Ken managed to hit the deck and, sliding from the pavement edge onto the roadway, stuck his outstretched foot into the spokes of the front wheel. The cyclist had no chance of dismounting and the sudden stop threw him over the handlebars in a steep dive, to land with a sickening thud, headfirst into the roadway. Ken jumped up and braced himself for more action, but the rider stayed down, and a quick check confirmed, despite his wearing a helmet, he had broken his neck. Peeling back his black, woollen, face mask revealed the dead man's Chinese features. Pocketing the would-be assassins' gun, he ran from the scene and didn't stop until he was a few streets short of where he and Kat were staying.

"Well that proves that they are on to us and we will

have to take more precautions and offer a lower profile in future."

"You're right Kat. Who would have thought it, an assassination attempt in sleepy Adelaide? But I guess the use of a bike rather than a car or motor scooter was in tune with Adelaidean niceties. It's time for a conflab with George, Chow Lim and the boys."

George was as inscrutable as ever when hearing what Kat and Ken had to report. He denied knowledge of the underwater weapons research but was more interested in the possibility of Chinese infiltration of Adelaide's defence research academia.

"It's clear that you are both potential targets, but we still have too little proven evidence to outmaneuver the Sinophiles in political and media circles, which is necessary for us to put our people in the field. But you must take more care of your personal security and I recommend you go armed from now on and have Pete's boys guard your backs. As far as the university situation goes, Chow-Lim should be able to help us there as he did in Melbourne"

"Thanks George, I agree that Kat and Ken need to lie low for a while and I can help, as there are a couple of Phd students working on the Submarine project research who are more loyal to Australia than China. One in particular, came here to study on a temporary visa basis, but as she progressed and moved into postgraduate, research she was successful in obtaining Australian citizenship and her family has come out to join her. I will find out what she suspects and get back to you."

16
TWO-WAY SPY

Professor Liao Tsang was very, happy with his job and comfortable life in Adelaide. He and his wife lived in a fine house in leafy, Unley and their son was a high achiever at the prestigious St Peter's College. He particularly valued the quiet conservatism of his locality and Dunstan's legacy was a polite acceptance of foreigners and especially well educated and cashed up Chinese. Through educational endeavour and achievement he had risen through the Chinese cadres and as his father had been sufficiently dedicated to Mao, he both survived the cultural revolution and was allowed to come to Australia to study and pass his knowledge back to his motherland. In Australia, his ability and hard work achieved professorial rank and he was considered a world class expert in sub-sea sonar, derived from his specialist study of whales and their communication techniques. He had published widely and continued to supervise both Australian and Chinese prospective PhD students. Though he had been granted Australian citizenship, he still held warm feelings for his birthplace.

Wendy Wong was a PhD student under his supervision, dedicated to improving the ability of underwater vessels to avoid sonar detection. She was more interested in the applications of the work she did under her tutor than its pure biological value and she was charged with maintaining the secrecy of her findings when they appeared to have military applications.

"I am very impressed with your work Wendy, but I note that you omit to reference the source of many of your critical findings."

"Yes professor, I take your point but as you know I am constrained by the rules of my contract with the Department of Defence Science from sharing what they consider to be of strategic value."

"Well, I appreciate that, but it makes it hard for me to fully evaluate your work and accredit for Doctoral submission. I am planning to go on a research trip to the Ningaloo area of WA to study the giant whale sharks and I would very much like you to accompany me but only on the condition that you share your findings fully with me."

"That's too good an offer to refuse. I accept."

Adelaide under cover

"How did your trip up north go, Wendy?"

"It was good, major, and I made some useful findings in respect of inter-whale communication and the effectiveness of my sonar-avoidance strategies."

"Was the good professor helpful?"

"Yes, he was very attentive and very, interested in helping me with my work. But funnily enough we were not together for long because he left for further up north to explore another area near Karratha. It seemed strange as the intense shipping up there was likely to deter whales." Also, he seemed quite anxious that I should await his return and leave him to get on with his work, up there, alone."

"That's really interesting. What do you know about his background and origins?"

"I was meaning to raise this with you. Unlike me, he left China in good odour, because of his father's status, whereas several of my family members suffered and died during the cultural revolution. He is well regarded there, and he has been named as an elite 'Thousand Talents Scholar' by Beijing and he has links to China's National University of Defence, which is controlled by the Central Military Commission. So, I think some of his work must be deemed to have military application. It's for this reason I am doubly careful about what I reveal to him from my work. What amazes me is that our university authorities are aware of this and yet do not put any restrictions on him."

Baiting the trap

"Thank you Chow Lim. Looks like we need to find out more about the good professor and if necessary, put a spike in his wheel. We will get defence signals to monitor his Beijing communication and Pete can keep him under observation."

A few weeks of intercepting Lao's communications threw up nothing untoward and it was down to Pete to see whether he could unearth anything. It was immediately clear that if he was spying, he was adhering to 'Moscow rules'-especially going with the flow, varying his pattern and staying within his cover.

But Pete and his team were well trained and experienced in covert observation, in Belfast during the troubles. They knew, after a while, that they would have to provoke him into taking a misstep.

"Ken, can you get your journalist friend, Den, to launch some false news that is likely to smoke our guy out?"

Den was very willing to help and suggested that an article in an anti-Beijing newspaper aimed at Chinese residents in Australia, might do the trick. To be sure that Liao read it, Cindy Wong was primed to draw it to his attention.

When it came out, the article focused on hints of Chinese espionage in Australia's universities and stopping just short of defamation, caused an immediate stir amongst the diaspora. The professor changed his daily walk itinerary and knowing what he was looking for, Pete spotted the tell-tale chalk mark on a public toilet's door frame, that Liao had made to signal his deposit of a message.

A thorough search in the loo located a loose brick in one of the cubicles behind which a note had been secreted. It was whisked off to George, without delay, for the attention of expert code breakers.

"Well done to your guys, this is the real deal. I don't understand much of the technical detail but it is clear that he is passing on information on the possible military applications of the marine science research group's work. There is no reference to our drones and the mother ship, but it is clear from his travels up there that he is on the trail and, if not stopped, he will reveal our secret trials."

"Where do we go from here?"

"You can leave this to us, Ken, now that we have concrete evidence of his spying activities."

"What will happen to him? Is he likely to be charged and imprisoned?"

"Certainly not. That would tell his Chinese masters that he had been compromised and would needlessly embarrass the university and government bodies who had been at best unwittingly complicit in letting this fox into the hen house. I am confident that when he is confronted, he can be turned and will start to pass on information provided by us which will be credible to Beijing but designed to lead them astray."

"How can you be so confident George?"

"He has more to lose by continuing to spy for them than if he comes over to us. His comfortable lifestyle and cutting-edge work mean a great deal to him and he would not want situations to arise that would make he and his wife social pariahs and expel his son from his prestige school. Then he would have to return home in disgrace with terrible consequences for him and his family. I am sure he will see sense — gone are the days of firing squads and we have no gulags to send him to. But of course, he is not to know that and if he proves reluctant, the fear factor usually does the trick. You and Kat have done a great job and significantly degraded a dangerous spy operation without causing any public scandal and outcry. We are sure there are more infiltrations going on elsewhere and when we have rung Lao dry, we may have some leads for you to follow up. But, in the meanwhile, take a break but don't forget that you are still targeted, and you should not lower your guard."

17
THE DRAGON WAKES

Things quietened down after the drama in Adelaide and the west. Kat returned to her family home in new South Wales and Ken resumed his consulting role back at his Carlton office. A lunch with Jack assured Ken that the loose ends in Victoria had been tied up and that the antics of the newcomer Chinese had been brought under control, courtesy of subtle warnings from appropriate power figures in the Federal Government and police.

"Thank you for what you and Kat did. I appreciate it was small beer compared with your subsequent achievements and yes, I know that you can't tell me anything about them. Your fee has been deposited in your bank account and it was agreed between the factory owners and others whom you helped, that a bonus was in order."

"Thanks Jack. As the saying goes, 'man cannot live by bread alone' but my patriotic duty is not sufficient to live off."

"Dead right, and a similar financial reward has been awarded to Kat. Thanks mate and keep in touch."

"Be seeing you Jack."

Bested by the bush

In the weeks that passed there was no news of espionage

scandals and ken assumed that George had been right, and that Lao had been recruited quietly and without fuss. Spring was on its way and Pete readily accepted Ken's invitation to join him on a road trip to the Flinders Ranges. Pete was good company, a more than competent bushman and provided a security back up that was unobtrusive and didn't cramp Ken's freedom too much. They had packed swags and other camping gear in Ken's Range Rover and Pete added a bag of goodies that he described as his insurance policy.

The freezing cold night was made bearable by the skilfully built log fire and coffee interspersed with sips of smoky Laphroaig malt whisky.

"Don't know about you Pete but being out under this carpet of stars takes my mind off the worries and stresses of the secret life."

"Even when I was out on dangerous reconnaissance missions behind enemy lines, the wonders of nature seemed to dominate the moments of apprehension and fear. The amazing sunrises in the Afghan mountains brought on a feeling of peaceful awe before the deadly cat and mouse game against the Taliban began again."

"Let's make the most of it because I fear our Chinese friends still plan some retribution and even in this fastness, we need to maintain our vigilance."

"I agree and you can rest easy tonight as I have strewn electronic motion detectors around our camp site and anything or anyone approaching from a couple of hundred yards out will tip us off. Our swags are sheltered by a rocky outcrop and away from the firelight's glow so even a sniper will be unable to target us at a distance."

"Sleep tight, Pete."

"It's amazing how the pioneer influences from the copper mining days are still in evidence. This Cornish pasty is the real deal. Savoury at one end and packed with sweetened apple at the other. I'm glad we decided to make our final lunch stop here at the Blinman store."

"The owners are really friendly too, Ken and chatting with them I learned that heavy rain further north will soon make the Parachilna river impassable and so we had better be on our way, if we are to get back to the main north-south highway."

"It would be a pity to get stuck and miss out on our booking at the Prairie Hotel. I have very fond memories of their feral mixed grill. First time I tasted crocodile and camel meat."

The road back to the highway presented little challenge to the powerful Range Rover but, to be on the safe side, Pete waded out ahead at the first crossings of the Parachilna, wielding a tree branch to test its rising depth and feel for dangerous obstacles under the swirling water. It was deemed safe to cross but the rapidly rising level warned of a neck and neck race ahead to safely pass the final river obstacles.

"It's starting to get hairy Ken. We had better get a move on. There are tyre tracks from a previous party but otherwise the gorge seems empty and there will be nobody following now to pull us out if we get bogged."

The clang of the bullet ricocheting off the car's fender sent Pete into a mad scramble to get aboard as Ken gunned the motor and raced up the road seeking suitable cover.

"So much for our being alone out here."

"Yeh. Famous last words. Better pull off the road at the top of the bend where we can get some cover and see where the shooter is."

From the vantage point on top of the spur, they had a panoramic view back along the gorge and Pete's powerful binoculars helped scan the terrain where the sniper was located. He was well hidden and another shot, which smashed the side window of their vehicle, proved that he was holding an advantageous position.

"Bugger. That was close. Time to dig into my bag of tricks and see how we can even the odds against us."

"We can't take too long about it, or we will be cut off by the rising flood."

"No worries. I have just the thing and it always works in these situations."

The drone that Pete released climbed swiftly and silently, scanning the ground as it circled above the gorge's rim. A clear picture of the terrain appeared on the control tablet in Pete's hands.

"Can't spot him yet. How about you mount your hat on a stick and raise it above the car's bonnet. That should give us a fix on him when he fires at it."

Ken did as was asked and his hat was blown away by an instant shot. The swooshing sound from the drone coincided with the crack of the rifle and ended with an explosion by a rocky outcrop, hundreds of yards up along the road. This was followed by cries of consternation and the roar of a vehicle as it took off on the road ahead.

"Thanks Ken. Got a clear view of him when he fired

and now that's one less to deal with, if we can catch them before the river floods us in."

"Great stuff Pete. Love your toy. Now jump in and we'll get after them."

"I'll put up the drone to keep a look out ahead and ensure we are not ambushed."

There was no time to admire the wondrous scenery of million years old rock strata as they charged along the road in pursuit of their attackers. The drone soon further proved its worth when Pete warned that two Chinese men were standing on the roof of their vehicle which was doors down in the swirling river. They had equipped themselves with a capable four-wheel drive, but their lack of local knowledge had caused them to pick a vehicle without a snorkel exhaust system and their precipitate entry to the river crossing had undone them.

"Bugger! They have shot down the drone. Prepare to stop in about a kilometre. We can look down on them from there and force them to surrender."

The Chinese were hopelessly exposed on the roof their wallowing vehicle, which showed signs of being swept away in the swirling current of the rain swollen river. But they had not given up and instead of responding to Ken's call for them to throw away their weapons and allow Pete and Ken to rescue them, they began to shoot.

"They are crazy Pete, or hopelessly brave. They are sitting ducks on the car roof and if they fall off, they have a slim chance of surviving in that torrent."

"Too right Ken, but if they don't give up soon the car will be swept away and they will not survive its passage through the narrowing gorge around the bend. I'll put a few warning shots over their heads and hopefully that will bring them to their senses."

Another gem from Pete's bag of tricks was a Heckler and Koch HK417, a favoured weapon of the Australian Army's specialist marksmen, which allowed him to ensure great accuracy at distances of up to six hundred metres. His first shot punched a hole in the car's roof and his follow up pierced the backpack one of the men wore. But even this did not deter them, and they continued to fire back until their vehicle was freed from the riverbed, spun around and disappeared round the bend.

"Well, we tried but I'm afraid their crazy brave stand will have cost them their lives."

"You're right Pete, they can't survive in that flood and even if it were remotely possible, staying alive in this country without supplies is impossible. Let's drive on. Our snorkel will get us across the river and as soon as we are back within phone coverage, I will ring George and get him to send in a helicopter party to clean up what's left of the guy your drone took out and confirm that the other guys didn't make it."

Having arrived at the Prairie Hotel, wet and muddied, the hot spa tubs were sheer bliss and the exotic barbecue with several beers hardly touched the sides. George had agreed to organise the clean-up operation and invited them to join him back in Melbourne to review what had happened and what their next move should be.

18
STIRRING THE DRAGON'S BROOD

Kat was convinced there was more to be learned about Chinese involvement in the university sector. A demonstration by Chinese students at a Queensland university, in support of the Hong Government's suppression of protests and the surprising lack of intervention by the university's council, added to her interest in finding out more of what was going on.

She made a point of befriending Wendy Wong who seemed to know more than she had previously disclosed about Beijing's penetration of Australian universities; especially those involved in cutting edge research.

Over dinner at an Adelaide Chinese restaurant, Kat urged her to reveal more of what she knew.

"I have to be careful what I say Kat, especially since the exposure of professor Liao. I am not a supporter of the Beijing regime, but I don't wish to become a target. However, I will say that there are people sponsored by the People's Liberation Army working in more sensitive research areas than mine and our authorities appear either ignorant of this or possibly even complicit. I suggest that you turn your attention to areas of cybernetic and biological research."

"Those don't seem to be related?"

"They aren't yet, but advances in Artificial Intelligence research may hold the key to linking them. AI is the most competitive technological area and whoever dominates that space will be a global leader in commercial, communications and military applications."

"Thank you, Wendy. That's very helpful but also, puzzling and concerning. I will make some more discreet enquiries."

"You had better be careful. You are already on their radar and they will defend their toe hold without mercy."

"Yes, Ken and Pete have found that out recently."

Melbourne, ASIS HQ

"Welcome back guys and I'm so glad you came out of that Flinders Ranges encounter in one piece. The clean-up team found the wreck of the shooters' car further down the river but there was no sign of the remaining two. Their bodies were not recovered nor did the police find any evidence of their having emerged into communities close to the gorge."

"It was touch and go at times George, but thanks to Pete and his toys we were able to best them and get away unscathed."

"You were bloody lucky Ken and it's clear that from now on you are a marked man. Maybe it's time for me to take a more leading role. What do you think George?

"I think we should take a step back. So far you have done all the running in searching out the threat areas and maybe it's time for us to put out a lure and draw them into our trap."

"Sounds good George, but what could we do that would stir the nest and bring out the dragon?"

"I want you to work on that Ken, and I suggest we get together with Chow Lim and Den to come up with some options. Remember it's time we fingered the people pulling the strings and not just their foot soldiers."

Baiting the trap

"Den, you have been at a distance from our activities and you have observed their outcome, what are your thoughts on where we should trail our lure?"

"I think it's time to stop searching for the Chinese protagonists and concentrate more on smoking out the Australian power brokers who are protecting and profiting from Beijing's incursions. You should start with the age-old question — who benefits? And look for the money and influence trail."

"Spot on Den and based on where we started and Ken's meeting with Senator Baker, Victoria is where we should focus our attention. What do you think Chow Lim?"

"Victoria is certainly a hot bed of pro-China feeling. Especially in some government circles. It is true that they have been dealing with Beijing regarding investment and infrastructure collaboration and even going as far as to be tempted to sign up to the Belt and Road Initiative. Senator baker is an enthusiast but more of a useful idiot than a treacherous plotter. Apart from the government, there are business, media and university cheerleaders who should be considered."

We have already touched on universities, but as Wendy Wong suggests, there is more going on there that bears looking at. Let's consider their incentive. Most Universities would go broke without the vast increase in full, fee paying students, which are predominantly from mainland China. The Academics are dicing with a boom time business model that can only be sustained by more and more external investment. They have cut corners regarding the calibre of the overseas intake and diluted the standards against which graduation is assessed. This sustains growth in staff numbers and runaway building programs. Business executive salaries are being enjoyed by Vice chancellors, some academics are even taking back-handers to pass favoured Chinese undergraduates and more marginal faculties, especially in the social science and arts areas, are being propped up by the foreign rivers of gold.

Their other vulnerability is the vanity of research reputation. Again the capital influx enables them to enter research fields that might not attract government funding and here is a real danger in that they have collaborated with foreign academic experts in areas that are vital to defence industry suppliers and weapons development. Victoria is the centre of significant naval, aviation and even space support industries and we are aware that high level researchers, originally from China but who have become Australian citizens, are active in these technical areas, despite having links with organisations which are affiliated with either the PLA or the Chinese communist government. This is a target area for us."

"What about the business fellow travellers, George?"

"The obvious candidates are to be found in the mining, food export, tourism and property industries. They range from those with legitimate business interests in Chinese trade, to lobbyists, who are starting to infiltrate party constituencies and even have a toe hold in state parliaments. At least one senior party official has been exposed taking money from Chinese interests without fully declaring its purpose. Again, this is most apparent in Victoria."

"What about the media Den?"

"It's more a reflection of the takeover of some mainstream and almost all social media, by left-leaning, so called, progressives who are a product of an education system increasingly controlled by social reform warriors, bred in the let-it-all-hang-out sixties, than any overt, malicious intent. They have reanimated the corpse of extreme socialism by distorting the historical curriculum and undermining the social underpinnings of the family and religion."

"Gee, that's a wide playing field, where and how should we begin? What do you reckon Den?"

"The best starting point would be to touch on their key areas of interest and see what that brings out. Maybe a planted story along the lines of that which brought the professor in South Australia undone."

"I like that approach and let's adopt a two-pronged attack with both a false news story and the dissemination of fabricated rumour on a personal basis amongst the China boosters."

"Good thinking, Ken. While you work up those ideas I will see what I can do to stir the diaspora pot, which is far from all pro-Beijing and my contacts there may be able to help us twist the dragon's tail."

"Thanks Chow Lim, let's get back together when we have firm proposals and in the meanwhile be extra careful and mindful of our individual security."

19
BLINDSIDING THE DRAGON

Dye in the water

"I hear you have been doing some interesting work in the avionics field since you came back from Silicon Valley. You must be doing some things very well Nic, to break into that area so quickly"

"That's right, Alistair. I have found a sweet spot that fits my skills and I have assembled a small team, which has enabled me to gain some rewarding contracts with defence support companies: technically advanced work, not too hush hush and well paid."

"Wouldn't you have done better by staying in America, closer to the huge defence lobby there?"

"I could but I can't stand the current President and his government and so decided to come home, especially as we are taking a much more understanding approach to China. Also I am convinced that the future will be more Asian than American or European and with luck we might even become more aligned with and part of China's Belt and Road Initiative."

"That's a prospect worth considering, interesting and thought provoking. But I would caution you not to cut yourself off from American scientific advances. They may be a politically divided country but they are back on the moon and entrepreneurs, the like of Musk, are doing very well out of their involvement in plans to set up a lunar space station which, as it excludes the Russians and Chinese, might readily morph into a military asset."

"I take your point. But western scientific circles leak like a sieve and the Chinese are past masters at infiltrating their secret projects and stealing vital know how, which enables agile outfits like mine to accept work at the cutting edge, without the burden and cost of having to invest in original research."

"That's very smart. But you must invest, preferably with borrowed money, if you are to win the greatest reward in this field and get in from the ground up on the next wave of winners. For instance, I wonder whether you are aware of the interest being shown in cislunar space by the competing global powers?"

"I know that some Australian companies are working with the RAAF to develop means of applying artificial intelligence to command intelligence in the space between earth and the moon."

"That's right but that's not all that's going on. As you know my merchant bank is called on at times to invest with government in potentially risky but obscenely profitable projects and, as a result, I sit on secret development committees with scientists and the military. Recently, I became aware that a great break through has been made in this cislunar work and that the government is looking for reliable sources of finance to put the theory into practice. I do not understand the technology but judging by the excitement of the panel members, especially the

Military, it's a world beater and will give the US allies a more than head start over their rivals."

"Wow. That sounds exciting. But isn't it top secret and why are you sharing this with me?"

"Like you, I believe we in Australia should not put all our eggs in one basket and it's not treasonous to make a killing out of serving one's nation. I am working with a select group charged with attracting the necessary investment and one of the front runners, in which I have an interest, would be strengthened if it had someone with your technical credibility on its board. Perhaps you would like to think that over — it could be a real game changer for you and your start up."

"How did you go with Nic, Alistair, did he buy it?"

"Greed always wins out over scientific ethics with guys like him. Hypocrisy personified. Brought up by a banker father who bought him the best private and prestigious university education and lo and behold he decries capitalism, speaks favourably of socialism and basks in privileged wealth amongst the new money men of California. Dr Nic Darnley is quite brilliant but has no idea of life in the real world of business. You should have seen how he dressed to come to lunch at my club. I had to remove his baseball cap and get the steward to find him a shirt, tie and jacket to conceal his T-shirt, bearing the slogan: 'Capitalism Kills.'"

"Typical of the Facebook, Twitterati generation. But will he do?"

"Oh yes George. The dye is in the water and we shall soon see where it emerges."

"Thanks Alistair, you have been very helpful."

"Pleasure George. Anything to put a spoke in the Chinese wheel."

Beijing

"It seems the westerners have gained a lead over us in cislunar space. This is very worrying as it would enable them to see all we are doing whilst we fly blind. Our satellites would be at their mercy and we don't know what systems of surveillance they intend setting up in their proposed lunar station. Can we believe our informant?"

"Yes, Minister. He is politically naïve but technically brilliant and he has succeeded so far in his business thanks to the seed capital our Australian friends have set him up with. His whole future depends upon cooperating with us."

"Then you must find a way to get parties representing our interests involved on the inside of this project."

The Melbourne Club

"So, you have attracted a bite, Alistair?

"Yes, George and from a very, interesting source. It couldn't be more, true blue. Well established family with links going back to the first fleet and interests in Mining, pastoral property and media. A big fish indeed."

"Any sign of a Chinese connection?"

"Not directly, but they have done business there through exports of minerals and beef. The owner is part Chinese and lives on a huge Kimberley cattle station"

"So, it could be a totally legitimate approach without unseen hands behind any proposed deal."

"Yes, but it seems too much of a coincidence for them

to emerge so soon after we floated the rumours and you and I are too long in the tooth, not to be suspicious of coincidences in this game."

"How do you think we should handle things from here?"

"We don't want to scare the horses and so we should initiate the usual preliminary discussions whilst planting amongst the financial wizards someone with more devious intent than their appearance suggests."

Kat to the fore

"Here's your chance Kat, to take the lead. Ken has been too exposed already and in the boys' club of bankers and financiers a female aid will be seen, as little more than a secretary charged with meeting their every trivial whim. This will enable you to be neither seen nor heard as you drift in and out of their deliberations in pursuit of their errands."

"What am I expected to unearth?"

"Any serious Chinese interest and at least identify the most influential Australian controlling hand."

"When and where do I start?"

"Alistair will attach you to his staff. We will arrange the appropriate security clearances and at this stage you need not be armed, other than with your usual means of discouraging unwanted male attention. You start tomorrow when there will be a weekend party down on the peninsula. This will give you every chance to socialise, whilst figuring out who's who."

20
DRAWING DRAGON'S BLOOD

Lunatic Landings

In between golf and other social camouflage, the government appointed team met in serious conclave with the prospective finance donor's representatives. On the government side were credible and well-credentialed scientists and treasury hacks, backed by RAAF and USAF officers. A presentation by one of the latter explained the strategic importance of understanding and hopefully being able to counter what rival nations might be doing and intending in cislunar orbit.

"We are well-aware of the Chinese's successful landing on the far side of the moon and it is rumoured they might soon plan to establish a permanent presence in their own space station. Their space program is far more military with a civilian sort of overlay."

"Major, what leads you to this conclusion?"

"At the end of 2015, the Chinese military had a massive reorganization and they pulled space out of the general armaments department. Beijing created the Strategic Support Force, or SSF, that realigned space operations with electronic warfare forces and network warfare forces, which includes, but is not limited to cyber. All of the space infrastructure launch facilities and mission control facilities were transferred over to SSF."

"But couldn't this be just prudent reorganisation of the sort the US government is practising in opening up space contracts to free enterprise organisations such as Space X?"

"With respect Nic, you don't go to cislunar without the active cooperation and participation of the People's Liberation Army because, you're launching from Chinese launch facilities that are run by them and the majority of China's mission control personnel are also trained by the PLA. What are they doing out there? Is this to establish a military dominance? We simply don't know, because nobody has really used that volume of space for military purposes so far."

Of more immediate concern, however, which could have military implications, is their deployment of the Queqiao relay satellite to Lagrange Point-2. The satellite was deployed to maintain contact with their Change-4, which successfully landed the moon rover. It has potential military implications because a data relay satellite set far beyond low-Earth orbit and geosynchronous orbit makes the system significantly harder to target or jam. At the same time, as you have noted, NASA is pulling back from monitoring all activity beyond earth's orbit and it is US government policy to commission private enterprise to fill the gap.This is why we are talking to you gentlemen to share with us the risk and considerable rewards associated with the successful deployment of our new, revolutionary, space monitoring system.

My scientific colleague will address, in broad terms,

the capability of this development, but you will appreciate that it remains top secret and we will not be able to share details until such time as we have agreed to work together and you have signed the Official Secrets Act."

"Space isn't really about space" the scientist declared. "Space is about the information that transits over it or is gathered by it. Cislunar space is becoming overcrowded and it makes sense that the Chinese would be thinking about it as the next place to establish themselves."

"Professor, are the Chinese the only potential threat?"

"Not entirely, China and Russia have pursued an international partnership, centred around space capabilities. The Pentagon's National Defence Strategy identifies those two nations as great power competitors and the biggest threats to the U.S. military. The Russian Space Agency has entered into discussions with the China National Space Administration to pursue cooperative lunar exploration missions, beginning this year. The concerns raised by these missions have created a push for the United States to increase its focus on cislunar awareness."

"Have you done anything yet to counter these threats?"

"Although agencies such as NASA are already working with private companies on collision avoidance for satellites in lunar orbit, up until now it hasn't been an area of focus for the Defence Department. The Space Development Agency has been looking at this and they haven't really gone public with any details, but they've said they are looking at options for how to do cislunar space domain awareness. The agency was established last year to take a new approach to modernising space-based capabilities, especially to focus on space domain awareness, which includes being able to observe what's going on and hopefully deter nefarious activity. Pentagon officials are concerned about Russian and Chinese anti-satellite capabilities, as well as space debris and other objects that could interfere with U.S. systems."

"Accepting that you cannot reveal all about the counter measures you are proposing to implement, hopefully with our help, what does your system do?"

"We have developed a Lunaspacial Intelligence Dash-board or "LUNINT, centred on a graphically enhanced three-dimensional situational awareness portal that will derive precise coordinates of notable objects in lunar space and on the lunar surface. This will also provide a satellite constellation architecture to monitor cislunar spacecraft. This new lunar intelligence discipline will help the U.S. government keep tabs on advanced adversaries."

"Sounds great but, as a banker, I wonder what the pay-off is, what do you get out of it that is of real-world value."

"What is at stake here gentlemen, is situational awareness of activities such as space-based solar power and asteroid mining. The Air Force's responsibility is to detect what's going on out there and who's doing what. That means making sure there are no surprises lurking in space for our assets. It is with the financing and technical installation of this system, that we are seeking a partnership with people like you."

Scientific Advance

Kat came and went from the meeting room to deliver messages and documents and was able to take in the make-up of the respective parties. She noted from his radically different dress, more suited to a Silicon Valley Maccas than a four star hotel, that Dr Nic Darnley was a member of the bidding team, distinctive for another of his provocative T-shirt messages in support of the 'Occupy Wall Street' movement. As she passed, he caught her eye, and his trailing hand gave her backside a proprietorial pat. She studiously ignored this crude advance and was equally aloof to his lascivious leer, as she left the room.

At the close of the day's business Alistair was able to report that all had gone well in that the bait had been swallowed and that the masquerade of a government team, whose few legitimate members were outnumbered by talented but, temporarily out of work, Actors Equity members.

All beer and skittles

Over drinks and dinner, more social familiarisation was intended to cement the growing level of trust between the parties. Wine flowed freely, parties broke away from the main gathering to pursue games of chance and others sought to play more tactile, games with willing, female escorts, posing as members of the hotel staff. It was after ten o'clock when Kat responded to the call to bring some important papers to Nic's room. When she knocked on his door, he called her in and she was not surprised to find him wearing only a towelling bath robe and with two full champagne glasses in is hand.

"Thanks for that Kat. Come over here, join me in a glass of bubbly and perhaps we can get better acquainted. As the old saw goes *'all work and no play ...'*"

Kat complied with his invitation to sit next to him on the sofa but, before he could say more, his dressing gown fell open to expose his stiff and excited member. He became even more aroused and groaned with pleasurable anticipation when Kat reached across, taking a firm but velvety, grip of his cock, with her free hand. The brief encounter that followed filled her with satisfaction and his loud exclamations confirmed the sensory impact on him.

At breakfast the next morning, she asked Alistair whether the absent Nic had slept in.

"Oh no. He was unwell during the night and had to be treated by the house doctor."

"Nothing serious I hope."

"Between you and me, my dear, I suspect the result of some nocturnal misadventure. According to the nurse attending the doctor as he inserted the stitches, he had never seen such severe lacerations in a man's pride and joy. It was as though it had been mauled by an animal's claw or savaged by an eagle's talons. He bled profusely and has gone home to recover. His team leader was far from impressed and I suspect we will see a lot less of him in future, if at all."

"Ah well. One down and I wonder how many more to go?" She mused, as she brushed a small fleck of skin that she had failed to detect behind one of the steel, prosthetic finger nails, that had replaced those ripped out by brutal Russian-backed, IRA torturers, when she and Ken exposed their terror trails.

Wrong side of the moon

Over ensuing weeks the parties met more and more frequently and were able to reach a complex and comprehensive agreement that saw $60 Billion paid to the government in return for the exclusive commercial rights and profits from the sale and installation of the cislunar surveillance system, when adopted by approved and extremely grateful allies.

"Well done our team. The five eyes monitors have already picked up attempts to break into the secure computers, where the cislunar strategy material is housed, by offshore players who are clearly of Chinese origin. We have reeled them in; exposed a most important Chinese agency and we have the means to take them out of the game. But I believe there is more to this than meets the eye and we still have to detect the Svengali who is directing Chinese subversion of our interests."

"Thanks George. We couldn't have done it without the help of Alistair, Den and Choi Lim and of course Kat's 'fingering' of one of the suspects. I suggest that we don't divert our energies to go after whoever that person is but continue to expose others who may lead us to the ultimate master mind."

"Agreed. Where should we turn next?" Kat reminded them of the suspicions voiced by Wendy Wong.

"What about ethnic weapons research?"

21
VIRAL INVADERS

King's College, Cambridge

Attending dinner on the high table at Kings was both a welcome treat for Porton Down's chief virologist and a valuable source of scientific gossip. As head of Britain's leading centre for research into chemical weapons and deadly diseases, professor Bright felt the weight of his responsibility to protect against these dangers and had to be ever alert to the latest rumour of potential threats. The chance to catch up with some of his university contemporaries, who comprised the elite of Britain's biochemical expertise, was particularly valuable both at a social as well as professional level.

"Although I am nearing retirement and it is so long since I supervised your doctoral work, Charles, I will never forget how you managed to keep abreast of the latest in both science and science fiction, without confusing the two and yet ever alert to improbable future applications. I expect that is why you hold the position you do."

"In these days of runaway technological advance and the increasing ingenuity of both major powers and underground enemies to dream up and deploy deadly, threats, it is only the long stop of a wild imagination that stands between us and an innings defeat."

"Do you still wield the willow for your village team?"

"Alas not as much as I would like. A combination of work demands and increasing arthritis in my hands frustrates me."

At the end of a delicious dinner, lubricated by the finest of selections from the college's extensive cellar and spiced with challenging debate, Charles was invited to retire to his former tutor's rooms for a night cap and more private conversation.

"I wonder Charles, whether you recall the work the Israeli's started and abandoned into ethnic weapons research!?"

"Oh yes, the controversial Ethno Bomb, designed to target ethnic traits found amongst Arabs. It was probably a hoax and probably more akin to science fiction than serious weapons research. Robert Heinlein's novel, *Day After Tomorrow*, featured a radiation weapon specified to attack pan-Asians only."

"The Russians are still taking it seriously and at one time they banned the export of Human bio-samples, fearing that they could be used to develop bioweapons targeting the Russian population. But, what I really wanted to discuss with you and perhaps alert you to, is a suggestion I have picked up from a Chinese student's Phd research work that Australian scientists are working secretly on developing an ethnic specific bio-weapon."

"That's very interesting and not entirely fanciful, they are not limited to cricket as they have several world class scientists and eight Nobel Prize winners in Physiology or

Medicine. If true it would really spook the Chinese, hence one of their students getting wind of it. As you know we have close relations with the Aussies, but they have no known research-centre comparable with ours. It doesn't ring any alarm bells for me but thanks for the reference and I will put out some feelers to see if anything like that is stirring in the Antipodes."

England, Porton Down, Wiltshire

"How was your dinner Charles?"

"As indulgent as usual and also, very useful. I had confirmation the rumour we started about the Australians working on an ethnically focused bioweapon has gained legs and is now being spread by a notable scientific gossip. It will not be long before it reaches the ears of the appropriate people in Beijing.

Melbourne, CSIRO

"We really are honoured to be receiving a visit by the head of Porton Down. He's a well-known cricket tragic and might only be here for the world cup matches. Otherwise we will learn nothing from him. Those bioweapons pommies are as tight as an oyster shell when it comes to sharing secrets about their work, and we have nothing of equal interest to trade with them.

"It's very good of you minister, to invite me out, coincident with the cricket, but I suspect you will want your pound of flesh in return."

"Too right Charles. Just a bit of PR work and lots of indiscretion over beers-if I recall aright, you distinguished yourself in that area when you were last here and your team won the test series."

Not just cricket

"I appreciate the atmosphere at Lords, cucumber sandwiches, the long room and all that, but I do admit there is nothing quite like watching a day night test in a corporate box at the MCG with the window open on a balmy, Mediterranean night. Food and drink's not bad too, especially your superior Victorian reds."

"Yes, it's great and such a pleasure to catch up with some one of your repute in the scientific world."

"Likewise, Professor. From what I hear you are no slouches in Canberra and your Defence Research people are world class."

"Too right and by the way the name's Bob not professor — we're a bit less formal down here. Can I call you Charles?"

"Absolutely — but never Charlie. My mother would have a fit."

"Forgive me for talking shop and I'll be brief. Rumour has it in scientific circles here that you might be out to discuss a collaboration with some of our blokes on a break-through in ethnically focused bioweapons. Before you answer, be assured I have worked closely with Defence Science on a number of ventures and I am a signatory to the Official Secrets Act."

"Can't say much about that here. Loose lips and all that, but if you might be interested in a role for you and a specialist team from your university, let's get together when I come to Canberra next week."

22
FERMENTING FALSE NEWS

The Melbourne Club

"Good choice for a meeting George, suitably under the radar or should I say hiding in plain sight, and the traditional English breakfast is sheer delight right down to the properly steamed black pudding and hand- made Roesti potatoes; no packaged stuff here. I see they even have white Boudin sausage on the menu as well."

"I knew I couldn't get your full attention over just a latte and a croissant. Tuck in and listen to what I have to tell you. The second lure is in play and we are working with the Brits, this time. They are providing scientific support and five eyes intelligence back-up."

"Sounds good and I am I right in assuming that fellow Cambridge man we met at the cricket is in on it and I bet he wasn't just a choral scholar at Kings?"

"Yes and no dunce — double first with distinction in the science tripos, a PhD at MIT in the states and now the head of research at Porton Down."

"Yep! No flies on him. What's the deal and where do Kat and I fit in?"

"There are two strands of malign influence we hope to expose and neutralise with this exercise in deception.

The first is the gullible and greedy scientific community and the second is the China-loving media. A leading university professor has made contact with Charles Bright, already, and is very keen to get involved with the ethnic weapons project. We are not sure whether he is a glory hunter, seeking just prestige and lucre for himself and his university, or an agent for Chinese interests. Professor Liao Tsang, the guy you helped us turn, will be useful here in that he can suss out any link between this academic and Chinese intelligence."

"What about the media angle?"

"This is where you guys can help. Amongst the media favouring a green-soft left line, there is a distinct willingness to apologise for Chinese doings here. Get in touch with Den and seek his advice on the most fertile avenue for the planting of rumour and how best to do it. You and Kat are not seen to be part of this scientific world and hopefully can gain acceptance without suspicion."

Feeding the Fourth Estate

"Hi Den, good to see you again. I guess George has briefed you about what we are looking for."

"Likewise, you certainly have been successful in pushing the Chinese challenge up the government's agenda and I am pleased to be able to stick a spoke in the wheel of our worst, false, and slanted, news purveyors. Broadly speaking the journos most likely to pick up on your information drop will be the ABC and commercial current affairs programs, dedicated to shock and awe, regardless of the collateral damage they do, such as the catastrophic impact of the live cattle exposé, on the national cattle industry and Indonesia's food supply. In addition, there are a number of unapologetically, soft-left rags that lust after leaks such as those provided by the infamous whistle blowers, Edward Snowden and Julian Assange. I can help you identify the likeliest targets but how to gain their attention is down to your ingenuity."

"I guess any direct conduct is likely to backfire but where do they pick up on most of their leads?"

"That's right Kat, but what you have to realise about the news profession is that their members are increasingly, younger, lighter on experience and under such pressure to be first with exclusive news to feed the voracious twenty-four hour news cycle, that they are more apt to go to print on unsubstantiated rumour than solid evidence. Their editorial mentors are equally less stringent in filtering out rumour and prejudice and basically follow, the apologise for errors later, tactic, rather than wait for informed permission. They certainly fly in the face of the famous dictum of the *Guardian's* great editor, CP Scott, that 'Comment is free, but facts are sacred'. You will have to feed your leak into the places they go, to pick up their clues. You will not find them in Libraries or out there where it's all happening, 'in real time'. The farthest many of them travel is by moving their fingers across the keyboard to interrogate Google and to join a close circle of like-minded colleagues and friends, in the heady world of the inner city latte lounges. Unless the currently defunct AAP is resurrected by a right-minded owner, that source of more reliable news is no longer a restraint on their scooping excesses."

Backed by your peers

In the scientific world, most of the 'latest' news of discoveries and advances is revealed to the outside world through scientists' breakthrough articles, whose only verification is more often than not a review by their peers or, in other words, supported by a circle of mates who are in furious agreement with them about their discovery.

"It's good of you to spare us the time, Charles. What we need your help with is mocking up some scientific articles that hint at breakthroughs in Cislunar intelligence monitoring and Ethnic weapons research, all supported by credible sounding reviewers."

"We spend much of our time at Porton Down sorting the wheat from the chaff in scientific publications and putting together spurious but just credible reports of valuable findings, will be meat and drink to my people. They will enjoy defrauding the more pompous and dangerous members of our fraternity. Consider it done. You might also get your military colleagues to do the same with revelations in the notable Defence industry journals and those periodic reviews of your military capabilities that appear in the Australian. I will have a word in George's ear suggesting the right kind of focus to attract the friends of our competitors and enemies."

Inside latté land

Close to Sydney's Ultimo and South Melbourne head-quarters of the ABC and in the green-left voting constituencies of the inner city, where many of the Journalists live, is an abundance of excellent, coffee dispensaries, which are hives of buzzing conversation.

But sadly, unlike the original coffee houses of London, Amsterdam and Vienna, they are more known for preaching amongst the converted than challenging and constructive debate. It probably explains why so many of the TV panel experts are, more often than not, in furious agreement with each other and rarely is a contrarian voice heard without its owner being derided and talked down.

Chow Lim had done a great job in planting a number of his science student connections amongst the eager news hounds.

"If control of this Cislunar orbit you are talking about is so vital to ensuring the safety of vehicles flying in that space and avoiding essential communication and navigation satellite collisions, why are our developments being kept top secret and not shared with the world?"

"That's right Emily — how can we have global peace and reconciliation of our differences if we practice one-upmanship in that area and especially when the military seem to have a hand in it. I think this is worth follow up and could make copy for an interesting article and maybe even a documentary on the box."

The topic got a full run amongst the patrons, but none of them considered that the Chinese were heavily involved in achieving potential dominance with their already landed rover on the moon and their intention to build a permanent manned space station there.

Elsewhere, in another patisserie within Sydney's 'goat's cheese curtain', the conversation about the horrors and ethics of chemical and biological warfare was in full swing.

"As if that COVID-19 pandemic wasn't bad enough, are

you telling me that Australia is dabbling with weaponising that sort of thing? If so, that's unconscionable!"

"It's even worse than that. What you are talking about is bioweapons designed to kill or disable only specific races and I suspect ours would be focussed on the genetics of Asians. But that's fantasy land stuff. Wasn't it featured in a science fiction novel?"

"That might be so but, not that long ago, it was believed that the Israeli's had perfected just such a weapon to disable people with Arabic traits. It was never proven but I can assure you the talk in Defence science circles is that our people are collaborating with Porton Down to develop one."

"This is terrible. The public needs to know more about it and it should be reported to the war crimes commission. We ban nuclear weapons, but this would kill a far wider range of people across a country and would have no anti-dote. If we can't stop it, we can at least ensure it is no longer secret and the Chinese need to be forewarned."

The false news seeds had been planted, watered with copious organic lattes and fertilised with layers of smashed avocado.

Canberrra, Press gallery lunch

Charles Bright delivered a master class speech, laced with information delicately clouded with subtle obfuscation. He waxed eloquent about the virus defeating work of Porton Down and its role in anticipating and combating bioweapon threats. His talk ranged widely, and despite the torrent of words, told his journalist audience absolutely nothing of what he really did at Porton and what was really happening with research into first strike bioweapons. The number of questions about ethnically targeted developments confirmed that Kat and Ken's disinformation work had been totally effective in reaching the right targets.

Later in his Canberra hotel suite, Charles met again with Professor, call me Bob, Jones.

"Thanks for travelling to see me, Bob. I know how demanding it is to be the head a major science faculty, especially in these straitened times for university finances and you must have a great deal on your plate."

"Think nothing of it, Charles. If what I hear you may be working on is true, the benefits that will accrue to Australia and our allies will be incalculable. At the same time, involvement in the work would add immensely to the reputation of my university and my faculty. It goes without saying that there would also be financial benefits that would go a long way to repairing the economic damage done by the post COVID-19 financial collapse."

"You will appreciate that at this stage I will neither deny nor confirm what we are working on and that anything we discuss here is under the confidentiality conditions of the Official Secrets Act. Should we progress work of the nature you have hinted at, we would certainly need all the help we could get from the best available talent and, if you will forgive my having made discreet enquiries about you and your team, I am assured that you would fit the bill. That's really all I can say at this stage but when our project scope is clearer, and the budget confirmed, I will be sure to be in touch. I can assure you, however, you have not wasted your time in putting yourselves forward."

"Thank you, Charles. I could have hoped for no more. But I am delighted to hear of the possibility of inclusion and be assured I will await patiently for future developments and, in the meanwhile, keep my mouth firmly shut."

Canberra, ASIS Headquarters

"Talk about the biter bit. The media is full of stories, mostly with an anti-government policy twist, about our supposed Cislunar triumph and our bellicose intentions in developing bioweapons designed to disable the Chinese.

You have done a great job and, to put the icing on the cake, Liao Tsang has confirmed that dear 'dinky di', Bob Jones, is up to his eyeballs in conspiracy with Chinese interests, such that, without finance from Beijing, his faculty would have been wiped out in the university reorganisation and retrenchment program. Also, he has a tightly knit insider trading syndicate arranged with some of our leading 'loyal' entrepreneurs, who are dangerously exposed to a shell company, which is heavily committed to share holdings in ventures he suggests will benefit from defence work and technical advances. Already, major cash advances have been obtained from Chinese investors and the syndicate, on good old Bob's say so, has plunged all of it on companies likely to gain from bioweapons research and development. If the project does not materialise, they will be ruined and goodness knows what retribution Beijing will impose on them.

Meanwhile, PLA cyber-warriors are flat out trying to hack into the Ethnic weapons research data. Alas for them they are making little progress because their target is non-existent and therefore theft proof. Also, many key media company and journalistic reputations are riding on their exclusive exposure of these so called undesirable, profligate, and unethical projects. They have so inflamed public opinion, that they will be unable to deny their accusations and retract their stories, without massive damage from legal actions when they are proved to be wrong."

23
SCORCHED BY THE DRAGON

ABC Breaking News

"Beijing has imposed tariff increases and direct embargoes on Australian exports in response to news reports of Australia's boosting of weapons research. Chinese students will not be able to attend universities here and the Royal Australian navy is tracking a Chinese battle fleet which is cruising off our northern shores and conducting live firing exercises."

"Strewth Kat. They have wasted no time in registering their disapproval of the initiatives we have orchestrated to slow down and deter their interference here."

"I guess we should take it as confirmation that we have really twisted the dragon's tail. But you know, Ken, the word from our Five Eyes China watchers is that they are confident of being able to hack into Defence Science's systems and steal the critical Cislunar intelligence and bioweapons developments."

"But they must be pretty pissed and even though we have adopted a lower profile lately, we must still keep up our guard. Our intelligence services have warned off the Chinese agents, who launched the previous attacks on us, but I fear that their local proxies, that we have spotlighted, might send some home-grown talent after us. So, take care."

Black Spur beat up

Ken was enjoying a spin, up over the black spur on the way to a relaxing weekend in Marysville, which had recovered sufficiently from its bushfire devastation, to restore many of its previous get away delights. Nothing could dampen his soaring spirits when he heard the bell birds tinkling calls, echoing off the hills and savoured the rich, eucalyptus, aroma wafting through his car's open window. At the crossing of the divide, he pulled into a welcome rest area, where he could relieve himself and sit for a while in the mild restorative sunshine. But, as he strolled back from the toilet block, he noted a cluster of parked Harleys and three tough-looking bikies, complete with leather club jackets and bike helmets, leaning against his car.

"G'day guys. Enjoying a spin in the clean crisp Victorian mountain air. Must be very refreshing after the Gold coast steam bath."

"Cut the cackle you pommie smart arse, or we'll hurt you even more than we've been asked to."

"What? Three midgets like you. This is mountain men's country here mate. We don't bulk up on bananas and drink that piss, pretending to be beer, you stole from Castlemaine."

While he wound them up, Ken considered what he was up against. He would have to separate them to have a chance and take on the biggest first. The absence of others in the carpark was to his advantage, as it would not inhibit his tactics. He had left his pistol in the car's glove compartment, but as far as he could see his adversaries were armed only with a selection of baseball bats, a tyre iron and a wicked looking machete. His moment of reflection lost him the element of surprise and in response to their rush attack, he ran away towards the surrounding trees, firing a rescue beacon into the air before they could close on him.

The biggest and ugliest arrived first, swinging his machete, as if he were about to cut sugar cane. Ken's only response was to extend the retractable police baton he wore concealed in a sheath inside his leather jacket. Stepping inside the swing of the machete, he delivered a bone crunching blow to the bikie's knee and the resounding crack, as the fibreglass coated steel baton shattered bone, confirmed that he would no longer be a threat. The second assailant paused a few feet from Ken, with a baseball bat raised to strike, when a shadow passed overhead and he fell to his knees struck down by a sling shot released from Pete's drone, that even his helmet could not withstand. There was no need to worry about the third one who hopped-around, howling and anguished by the cross bow quarrel that was protruding from his thigh. Kat had not lost the skill she had so ably demonstrated in a touch and go moment in St Petersburg, on their previous assignment. In short order, all three had been accounted for with a minimum of silent effort.

It had been a wise decision to prepare for the backlash and when Ken, Kat and Pete reviewed the success of their defensive strategy, they determined to keep it up against future threats. Of the injured bikie trio, only the one with the crossbow injury was in any condition to be interrogated about who had set them on. Even in his fragile state, he put up some initial resistance but a quiet session with Kat and the threat of what her steel fingernails could inflict, loosened his tongue but he had little to reveal. It was clear that they had been hired by local rather than direct Chinese parties but as they had employed an anonymous cut-out to brief and pay them, the identity of the éminence grise remained a tantalising secret.

24

DOUSING THE DRAGON'S FIRE

Breaking the bad news

"I have just received this disturbing communication from the Chairman of the government's Cislunar project:

'Dear Alistair

It is with considerable regret that I must advise you, that we will not be going ahead with the Cislunar communications project and this means of course that our contract with you is void.

Having completed a detailed audit of expenditure in relation to progress on the project, Treasury has advised us that it is unlikely to be commercially viable and although the technology is sound, should it go ahead in future, it could only do so with the complete support and finance from the five eyes partner countries.

We regret the adverse financial implications and effect upon those further partners you have contracted to join in the work. We can only assure you of our satisfaction with your approach and performance and that you are certainly on our list for future contracts of this nature.

Thank you for your considerable contribution to our security in space initiatives.'"

"Does that mean what I think it does?"

"I'm afraid so, Sir Eric, we have failed to capitalise on this contract and, even worse, we have not got to the stage at which we could gain full access to the technology."

"Our Chinese sponsors will be furious, but at least we should get back most of the considerable sum we sank into this dud. How much was it Alistair?"

"I'm afraid north of $30 Billion and even worse, we are unlikely to get any of it back."

"What do you mean-surely there was a force majeure, get-out clause in the contract that guaranteed financial compensation?"

"That's right sir, but when I rang them, the number had been discontinued and none of my government contacts had heard of this body, nor the Cislunar project. I fear we have been conned, big time. When news of this gets out, your financial soundness will come under question, your reputation will take a big hit and it will be disastrous for the technical sub-contractors who have hired expensive staff, facilities and equipment."

Before this calamitous news could be fully digested, their conversation was interrupted by a sharp rap at the door and the swift entry of a somewhat flustered, aid.

"Pardon me Sir Eric, I have just received a call from your stockbrokers. It seems some bad news about the Cislunar work has been leaked to the media and the shares of your family company have totally collapsed. What's more we are getting calls already from your bankers, sub-contractor companies and a Chinese government minister is expecting you to call Beijing, urgently."

"Christ almighty, Alistair, we are really in the shit. The

financial collapse is appalling but I am very afraid of what revenge the Chinese will inflict on us. Even worse will be the summons to front the boss in the Kimberley."

ABC News break

"News is coming in that one of Australia's wealthiest and longest standing, family business consortiums has lost a significant defence related government contract and their stock exchange standing is in free fall …"

Melbourne Club

"Alistair, what's going on? Have those government bastards welched on us? Can I get my money back?"

"Afraid, my boy, that it's much worse than that. We have been conned by someone posing as government representatives and you have certainly done your dough."

"But that can't be. You got me into this and encouraged me to take a big career risk for certain reward. This will ruin me. What are you going to do about it?

"Sorry mate. That's capitalism. You roll the dice and have to accept the numbers as they fall. You're a clever lad and maybe there will be something for you in the university sector. Must dash now I have a few problems of my own."

"God, what will I do? I have bet everything on this, borrowed to the hilt and dragged friends into it. I am ruined and my reputation will be rat shit. Hopefully, the Chinese will be too focused on Sir Eric's responsibility to take any action against me. Fuck capitalism!!"

Beijing, Viral Spike

"Minister, we have just received the alarming news of a severe outbreak of a deadly virus, of unknown origin, amongst our top defence officials and military officers. It's so serious we have called an immediate halt to our operations in the South China Sea and we have cancelled our harassment of Taipei and plans to post army units in Hong Kong."

"What do you mean by 'of unknown origin' surely those Australian dogs have not released their ethnic bioweapon on us?"

"No sir, as far as we can tell it is not targeted along ethnic lines, but it is new and we expect some careless leak is responsible, caused by those fool scientists in our chemical warfare laboratories. Strangely, though, preliminary analysis suggests it might be of north Korean origin."

"That can't be true. Kim Jong-un wouldn't dare, and he has no cause to attack us. It is vital that we shut this down completely to prevent an escape into the general population and prevent any word of it getting out. We can easily clamp down on the military and politicians. If necessary, those affected can be isolated in the remote labour camps near the Russian border. We have only just recovered from the reputational damage we suffered because of the Corona Virus leak. Another would be calamitous for our international face and you and I might not survive the fall out."

Canberra, ISIS Headquarters

"Five Eyes has reported total panic amongst Communist

party top brass in Beijing. Looks as though your shot has hit the bull's eye, Charles, congratulations, and thanks for your help. It was very clever of you and your people to release a debilitating, but not lethal, virus, which could not be traced back to us and contaminating Professor Bob Jones and members of his team, who transmitted it to their Beijing contacts, was a master stroke."

"My pleasure, minister, and my people back at Porton Down got a kick out of it and learned from the exercise. Of course we could not have pulled off the real deception of its having a North Korean origin, without the Americans passing to us some of Kim Jong-un's latest germ warfare samples and Chow Lim was really helpful in connecting us with our South Korean counterparts who were more than happy to help us give the virus a credible North Korean signature."

"We hear that top echelons of their defence ministry and military are badly infected, such that their war footing is faltering badly, and they are desperate to keep it a secret, after their Corona virus stuff-up."

"Will you now leak this to the international media and blow their credibility out of the water?"

"No, we will be far more devious than that .Once they know that we know about this viral leak, we can agree to keep mum in return for certain concessions and changed behaviours on their part and you can bet the North Koreans cannot look forward to much help from Beijing in future. We have blunted the threat of two aggressors with one masquerade. At the same time, the Russians will find out and it is sure to cool Putin's dalliance across their Chinese border."

"Great. That's a really huge bang for your buck."

"Thanks again Charles and as a small token of our thanks and esteem, here is a cricket bat autographed by the whole Australian team. Good to have, especially as your boys won the series and we intend taking the ashes back."

"Thank you Minister. We will be continually wary of the roo with the twisted tail"

Counting the cost

"What great outcomes George. Without spilling too much blood and treasure."

"Yes, Kat, our universities, businesses and media have burnt their hands very badly through their involvement and boosting of these pro-China enterprises and they will not be so keen to get involved in future.

Sir Eric's company and his reputation is shot for all time. Poor old Prof Jones is in trouble since Den leaked to the media news of a bungle at his laboratory, that infected his staff and needed CSIRO help in finding an antidote. His university is unimpressed, and his career is over. Sadly, the body of Nic Darnley was washed up on Bondi beach. The official finding was suicide, but special branch suspects a Chinese hand in his demise.

The unscrupulous, get-rich-quick entrepreneurs are running scared and those of their fledgling enterprises, which hoped to make it big at government expense, are empty, rotting shells. Den tells me that a number of Journalists and their editors have been reassigned to lesser roles or are to be retrained in proper journalistic practice and ethics, especially learning the difference between facts and opinions, or should I say biases? Most importantly of all, we have not just arrested the growth of Sinophile influencers and collaborators amongst our own, we have set back the cause of Chinese hubris and bullying for the foreseeable future."

"Another job well done, and our work is really over."

"You have both done better than I hoped and caused less trouble than I feared but I must remind you that there is still a master mind somewhere out there."

25
CONFRONTING THE DRAGON

Invitation to the dance

For the next few months Kat and Ken went their own ways: he attended to his neglected business and she returned to her family home. They maintained a degree of alertness to any personal threat and despite the diminished sense of danger they both went about armed. They stopped trying to find out who was pulling the strings of the Australian, pro-China push and enjoyed a more relaxed lifestyle. Ken checked in with George, now and again, but he had no news about their quarry.

Then, at the same time, both received a charming and intriguing invitation to be guests at a substantial outback cattle station, to attend the local picnic races and enjoy the celebratory ball that followed the racing of bush-bred horses.

Éire'
Kalumburu road,
West Kimberley
WA.

Dear Kat/Ken
I would be pleased if you would be house guests on

my cattle station which is in the wonderful outback, Kimberley country, along the Kalumburu Road, up near the Kalumburu community, which is one of the oldest and the most northerly Aboriginal settlements in Australia. I understand from business contacts in Victoria that you have both been conducting research for a book on rural life and I thought you might appreciate seeing the inside working of a substantial outback property.

If you were to come towards the end of this month, you could get acclimatised before the running of the nearby and quite famous picnic races and enjoy the ball, at my place, which celebrates the completion of the racing carnival. People come from all parts of Australia for the races and I will be hosting family and other friends who will welcome your company.

You won't be expected to work for your keep but as I hear that you were raised on a sheep property, Kat, feel free to bring your riding boots and join in the mustering. The size and business of the station is best appreciated from the saddle. If riding's not your thing, Ken, don't worry, there are fine shooting and fishing opportunities and we can provide the necessary guns and rods. In addition to all that, there are great examples of aboriginal rock art in a remote part of the station and a priest at the community is a mine of information about them.

I hope you will be able to come. Let me know when you will be arriving, and I will arrange for a pilot to meet you at Broome airport and fly you out here. This is preferable to the road trip at this time of the year as we have just come out of the wet season; not all parts of the roads have been regraded and some crossings of still flood swollen rivers can be dangerous.

Look forward to meeting you both.
Kind wishes,
Gloria Jane Maguire

Kat agreed with Ken that this was an opportunity too good to miss. The Kimberley was reputedly both beautiful and highly spiritual to the first people and it would be a unique and refreshing, experience for both of them. They agreed to meet in Broome and although the place was well established it was remote and Ken cautioned that they should still carry their personal weapons with them, ensure they had adequate coverage and advised, George, Pete and his mates, where they were heading.

Kimberley castle

The flight in the light plane from Broome to the station was more than just spectacular, as they overflew red-rock gorges, monsoon swollen rivers, plains of head-high grass and the mystical cones of Purnalulu. The pilot called out when they crossed the station's boundary and it seemed, as far as the flight from Melbourne to Sydney, before the homestead and bush runway came in site. The setting was truly spectacular with the main house sited on the lip of a deep, ochre coloured, rocky gorge with twinkling blue, river water flowing far beneath its vertical sides.

They were met by the station manager and driven in a work-scarred Range Rover to a handsome broken-back, roofed house, where they were to stay. They were met on the veranda by a tall, lean woman with the most amazing contradiction of fiery, red hair, lightly tanned skin and Asian eyes. Despite her disarming smile and welcome greeting, her handshake was firm, her roughened skin suggested she was acquainted with hard work and her penetrating look gave warning that she did not suffer fools gladly.

"G'day Kat and Ken! Welcome to Éire. Is this your first visit to the Kimberley?"

"Thank you, Gloria and yes, this is our first visit and judging by what we saw flying in, we are looking forward to getting out into your wonderful country."

"I can assure you Kat, that it will not disappoint and as well as the natural wonders you will be able to see mystical aboriginal rock art, especially the powerful Wandjina on the rock wall of a beautiful pool in a distant, secret, corner of my property. Now you must want to rest and clean up before lunch and my housekeeper will show you to your rooms."

Kat and Ken were the only lunch guests; others were out enjoying various activities and the meal was light and tasty.

Gloria was set on finding out all she could about them and Kat and Ken answered her questions to a degree but did not reveal anything about their clandestine activities.

"I hear you are a change consultant, Ken and specialise in working with dysfunctional teams, that might be something that could be applicable to some of my ventures. But you write books, too?"

"I do Gloria but that is more a pastime than a serious form of work and I have been trying to get under the skin of rural people and life in the bush to understand what makes country Australia tick."

"Feel free to interview me as I have lived and worked in the bush all my life"

"How did that come about?" Kat asked.

"I am the fortunate descendent of nineteenth century Irish drovers who opened up this land to grazing on a large scale and I have inherited a substantial cattle empire which supplies hamburger meat to our south and internationally. Also, we produce a special line of grain fed Wagyu and Black Aberdeen Angus beef, some of which you will be able to savour at dinner tonight."

"I hear that's not all you are involved in?"

"My father was astute enough to reinvest his profits in the good times and he got in at the ground level when Hancock found the first iron ore reefs in the Pilbara. We have two very profitable iron ore mines, interests in smelter coal and mineral sands, all of which are highly appreciated by our Chinese customers. You may think it strange in such a man's world that a woman should be in charge, but as my father died a few years back and my mother left when I was a child, I grew up riding and roping cattle, worked up from the bottom in the mines and consequently inherited all the businesses and chose to manage them. I have not chosen to marry and so this is my life and I seldom leave this place, except when it is necessary to visit the mines and my customers in Shanghai."

"I am impressed that you are so attractive and feminine, despite leading such a tough life and being exposed so much to this harsh climate."

"Oh, you are a charmer. Do I detect curiosity about my Irish hair and my oriental eyes? That's because of my parentage. It's no secret that when my father was prematurely widowed, he couldn't resist the charms of our Chinese chef's exceptionally beautiful daughter and I am the product of that union of two totally different cultures. The same is true of the history, philosophies and values, instilled in me as I grew up, by my father and Chinese chef grandfather, especially as my mother couldn't cope with the scandal of what she had done and committed suicide before I was five. I worshipped the ground he walked on, Irish myths and legends and tales of the high kings were my bedtime stories and I was tutored to admire the Fenians and even the more contemporary heroes, such as Bobby Sands, who fought and died for Ireland's freedom. You will understand from that, although I am a proud Australian, I am no lover of the English and their empire.

The same was true of my grandfather's influence, during many hours I passed in his kitchen and working with him to feed the stockmen, when out mustering. He taught me the principles of Confucius and told me of the heroism of Mao and those with him on the Long March. This combined upbringing and education in two cultures made me rather indifferent to tales of Captain Cook and the Anzacs.

That's enough about me. Tomorrow, Kat can get back on a horse and ride with me to see some of the herd and you Ken may ride the helicopter down into the gorge and see if you can catch some Barramundi for tomorrow's dinner. But be careful, sometimes the floods carry the salties up here from the sea and you don't want to become a croc's supper."

More than just beef

The riding was a great success. After a rusty start Kat demonstrated her comfort in the saddle and was even able to cut out a calf for branding. Gloria was very impressed and proved to be an excellent guide, sharing freely her hard-earned knowledge of the industry and the stockman's trade. At the end of the day there was less of a barrier between them and Gloria offered to put out a suitable dress for Kat to wear at the upcoming ball.

A fine catch

Ken had an equally informative and satisfying day. With the help of an aboriginal local, he was able to land a brace of very fine 'Barra' and was instructed in the many ways of traditional bush cooking that preserved the freshness and flavour and about the native herbs that added spice to the fish. A tasty catch, but an even more fortunate one was to cap off Ken's day. On the way back, his guide was so pleased by his eagerness to learn about all things aboriginal, he persuaded the pilot to veer off the main course and fly extra low to take in the Wandjina pool. The sight of the tranquil, shady billabong was worth the diversion and all was well until the pilot shouted with alarm and climbed as fast and hard as the copter could manage, just clearing a jagged rock ridge, to head safely for home.

Ken was smart enough not to ask about the strange looking, camouflaged, buildings, sunk into the desert sand and their strange array of antennas and dishes, that he spotted briefly as the chopper veered away and they dropped out of view behind the ridge.

High-roller races

The bush racetrack had little in common with Flemington. The surface was hard packed dust rather than grass and instead of rails, the circuit was ringed by oil drums. Nonetheless a substantial crowd had driven and flown in for the day. Food trucks fed the masses and VIP marquees catered for the champagne set. Ken was surprised to see so many well-known faces from mining, politics, sport and media and he was even more intrigued by the numerous and different groups of Chinese attendees. He and Kat made a point of mingling and sought out any opportunity to chat with the Asian contingent.

It was soon apparent that most of them were Gloria's customers, and a small, expensively turned out, clique of men and women were gambling high rollers, taking a break from Australia's top casinos. Most interesting was a cluster of much younger, nerdish types of Chinese heritage, who drank sparingly, bet little and seemed to be much beholden to a military looking type who finally mustered them and took them away in a series of dust-coated SVUs. Who were they and where were they going? Certainly not to the homestead and there was no other accommodation for hundreds of kilometres. Perhaps they had something to do with the secretive facilities Ken had detected, from the air.

He had smuggled a satellite phone in with his luggage

and took the opportunity, before dinner, to call George and brief him on their findings and suspicions.

The Chinese century

Dinner was served in the elegant, dining room of Éire's homestead. The table was very grand and replete with Victorian era napery, silver cutlery and Waterford crystal glassware, which sparkled and reflected light from the overhead chandeliers. The centre piece of the lavish dinner was the Chef's appearance to carve succulent slices from a Baron of Beef, mounted on a carvery trolley.

The diners comprised the elite of Gloria's guests and amongst them were two very mature and dignified Chinese men. One of whom was the purchasing director of her ore buying customer and a very senior commerce department minister from Beijing.

Although the dinner's style emulated one out of the house's Victorian past, its etiquette was right up to date and there was no separation of the sexes, nor cigars and brandy, only for the men. Instead, the Chinese official rose to deliver a vote of thanks to Gloria on behalf of her happy customers and the evening's guests.

"Mademoiselle, your dinner was as legendary as your achievements on behalf of your country and as a good and loyal friend to mine. The way in which you have expanded on your father's legacy, despite Australia's male dominated history, built up a considerable mining enterprise and retained your roots in this wonderful place, is truly astounding and highly commendable. Thank you and I and my colleagues look forward to reciprocating your hospitable, welcome, when you next travel to the new China."

Gloria nodded her head in appreciation and rose to reply. She wore a stunning, emerald green, shantung-silk, Cheongsam dress, which reflected both her heritages and accented her lithe, sensuous form. All faces turned to hear her with rapt attention.

"Honoured guests. Thank you for those too kind words and for undertaking the exacting journey to come to this remote and sacred place. As you know from the name of the station and my paternal origin, I am devoted to all things Irish and although Eire has not yet achieved its destiny of total freedom from the yoke of the English, please join me in recognising the miracle of the republic and drink a toast to its ultimate success. '*May the saddest day of her future be no worse Than the happiest day of her past.*'

But that is only half of my history and my association with and regard for modern day China is very much my present and future. Just as the adoption of capitalism with a socialist face, has lifted millions of her people out of poverty, China's investment and ever expanding uptake of our minerals and energy, has, like our earlier bounty of wool and gold, lifted Australia from the depths of mediocrity to our present elevated status in the world. This is truly China's century, as she shakes off the shame of exploitation by the European colonial powers, overpowers the ancient threat from Japan and faces down the world dominance of America.

I will continue to be an admirer and true friend to that celestial, country and I ask you all to raise your glasses again to toast the continued success of the middle kingdom and its ever closer ties with Australia. *Ganbei!*"

She sat down to unanimous applause and turned to look at Kat and Ken with a triumphant and far from friendly, smile.

Later that night, in the privacy of his room, Ken phoned George.

There is no doubt about it, George we have found the Dragon or should dare I say Dragoness, in this identity obsessed world. The ball will distract everyone tomorrow evening and amongst the crowds we will not be missed. We must go in tomorrow night."

26
BREACHING THE DRAGON'S DEN

Eye in the sky

The air force's new, unmanned, 'Loyal Wingman' drone, ghosted its way across the night sky, feeding back real time video streaming of the secret Kimberley compound, to its controllers at a northern airbase.

"All quiet down there, sir. The Buildings are extensive but not substantial. They seem to be relying on their remoteness, rather than solidity, as a key defence against any intrusion. There is a razor wire perimeter. No evidence of mines, but there could be some buried IEDs and whilst there appear to be no sentries there is a roaming pack of dogs. I'm no expert on telecommunications but, the size and number of aerials and discs, suggest a powerful communication capacity, maybe even with the ability to interact with satellites."

"Thank you, Lieutenant. Get the video recordings off to HQ as quickly as you can, and we will await orders about any further involvement that is required of us."

In Éire's back yard

In addition to the video coverage from the RAAF, Kat and Ken were briefed by Pete about what his boys had seen.

In true SAS style they had staked out the target beforehand, enduring the freezing cold nights and hot, steamy days, to spy on the comings and goings at the compound and testing its security to identify the potential access points.

"It's not as securely defended as a real military site but the size of its generators and all the aerial and satellite tackle suggest a huge power consumption, with the capacity to offer a number of nasty electronic traps for the unwary, would be intruder. We have the gear to probe into the buildings to see and hear what is going on and we have with us a couple of experts from ASIO who can make sense of their technology and translate speech from Mandarin and Cantonese. At a more mundane level, we can eliminate their Doberman guards without killing or maiming them."

"OK Pete, good job and how do you suggest we should gain entry with the minimum of force as we don't yet know for sure it's an illegal foreign gig?"

"First off, my portable drone can give the place another once over and drop baited meat that will put the dogs in dreamland for several hours. When that's done, we can cut through the wire, as there seem to be no electronic alarms nor trips to switch on arc lights. My boys best go first as they are used to stealthy approach methods and they have electronic devices that will detect any planted IEDS in their path. When we get close enough to the buildings, we can insert miniature cameras and we have the latest Israeli developed equipment that will feed back any conversations via the light bulbs in the rooms."

"Sounds great but remembering the old caution that

once battle is engaged, the best of plans can go out the window, what's our fallback in case we are detected and, as you cautioned, they do have some defensive surprises for us?"

"My team is heavily kitted out with all that is needed to sustain a major fire fight including, light mortars, armour piercing rockets and of course the dear little armed drone. Should it escalate beyond our capability, there are two Black Hawk helicopters standing by, and they are stuffed with the meanest assault troops that Australia can provide and enough firepower to sink a battleship and foil an air attack. If all else fails there is that newly acquired wonder weapon, the Loyal Wingman, circling unseen up above and which can do far more than just take pictures."

"You have convinced me we are all good to go, so let's get to it."

Inside the wire

Kat and Ken were dressed for combat and carried both Steyr rifles and automatic handguns. In addition, Kat had strung her lethal cross bow, across her back. Slithering in through the cut wire, their night vision goggles enabled them to see the prostrate dogs sleeping off the dreamy, heaven-sent, meal of doctored, eye fillet steak. Closing on the structures, the scouts signalled that the way ahead was mine-free and breaking into pre-arranged sub-teams they approached each building and began to insert camera probes and search out line of sight access points to read conversations radiating from the light bulbs. Ken and Kat found a suitable, central, observation point and set up communication kit that would allow them to receive and send pictures and sound to and from teams, via their tablet computers.

"Anything coming in yet, Kat?"

"Not much of interest in the first two huts, one looks like a store and the other a dorm, judging by the amount of snoring. Wait a minute. There's some real action in a separate room of the dorm. Wow, he's really giving her one and both seem very happy with the exercise."

"Ok stop recording tips from the porno show and focus on the biggest building where Pete is leading the listeners."

"Yeah, there is a lot of movement and voices. We just need to wait a little, while the interpreter gets back to us. Ok here he comes."

"K and K. We have hit the jackpot here. It certainly seems to be a very well-equipped control room and the technician says they could guide a moon landing with all the gear they have there. They are speaking in Mandarin and from the little I can understand, without being familiar with technical terms, it seems they are intercepting signals from somewhere and transmitting information up to a Chinese satellite orbiting to the north of Australia in cislunar orbit. Sounds like sufficient grounds for inviting ourselves to the party."

"OK. All teams, you are authorised to force entry but no shooting or heavy violence unless in self-defence."

The response was immediate. "OK, copy that. We are on our way. See you inside."

The assault on the buildings was a damp squib. At each one the intruders found the doors unlocked and the occupants shocked and bewildered at the sight of men, armed to the teeth, challenging them and calling them to surrender. The main building of interest housed an array of equipment, including individual screens for each of the thirty or so operators. Some of them reacted quicker than others and sought to turn off or disable their devices, but a quick burst of automatic weapon fire into the ceiling persuaded them to stop and submit to having their hands tied with plastic cuffs, along with everyone else on site.

"Have we got them all Pete?"

"I think so, at least all who are in these buildings, some may be doing outside work somewhere, and if so, the results of detainee interrogation and feed from my drone, which is scouring the surrounding country, will answer your question."

"First of all, as all the people seem to be of Chinese extract, have our translator calm them down and assure them that if they co-operate, they will not be harmed. Then we need to identify the leadership and question them about the purpose of this place and who is sponsoring it. Also, the technician needs to make a rapid assessment of what is going out and advise how we avoid giving away our presence to outside interests until we have government guidance. It could be that they may want to preserve the fiction of business as usual by feeding false information to an enemy."

The technician acknowledged this request and said that the scope of what confronted him would require considerable back-up by colleagues and that he would send a shout-out immediately, for more manpower resources.

As there was no sign of armed resistance, the back-up ground and air forces were stood down and George confirmed that ASIO was flying in a team to take over from Kat and Kim's strike force.

"All is under control here, Ken, but although the drone has not spotted any others outside, there are traces of a small party heading out beyond its range. Whoever it is must have planned for such a contingency, as they are using Camels rather than cars to get away, which will enable them to navigate the most hostile terrain and blend well into the surrounding country."

"Thanks Pete, well done. The interrogators need to find out who the escapees are and where they might be headed. In the meanwhile, You, Kat and I, need to get ready to follow them and not allow them to get away. They may be headed for a place where they can be extracted by air, so I will alert the Airforce to monitor any incoming, undeclared flights in this area."

"Before we leave, you should know that a radio message was sent out immediately before we moved in and it seems to have been received back at the Éire homestead."

In a shed, behind the cluster of buildings, they found a very capable all-terrain vehicle, designed for military use in that it had a light machine gun and grenade launcher mounted on the outer framework. It was fuelled up, contained jerry cans of spare diesel and plenty of water. It took a matter of moments for them to throw in their kit, personal weapons and rations. Then, having located the GPS satellite for guidance, they set off in pursuit of those who had got away.

The sunrise lit up the dull surrounding rocky ranges, turning them from muddy brown to a fiery orange, like molten steel pouring from a blast furnace. Soon, the heat, augmented by reflection from the rock surfaces, would blast super-heated, air across their desert way. It took them all day to sight the refugees. There were only three of them, mounted on two camels which suggested that they had pushed on so hard that one animal had foundered already.

When they were but a mile ahead, a light plane skimmed onto a flat stretch of gibber plane and readied itself to fly out the fugitives. Ken cursed and figured that he had been outwitted but, just as he thought all was lost, a menacing Apache helicopter loomed out of the shimmering haze and confronted the plane, presenting the deadly threat of its Hell Fire missiles and ferocious chain gun.

It didn't take Ken long to confirm that the three were high-ranking military communications officers who were secured along with the pilot and left on the desert floor to be collected by an incoming Black Hawk. But it was Kat's threatening approach that persuaded them to reveal that a fourth person, whose outback skills made them able to blend into the country, had peeled off back along their trail. It was clear that they had got away and the only option remained for them to await the larger helicopter and organise a lift back to Éire station.

27
DEATH TO THE DRAGON

Heart and home

Gloria appeared on the steps of the homestead to greet them. She looked cool and relaxed in a denim shirt and skin-tight powder blue, jeans.

"G'day Kat and Ken. Where have you been and what's with the paramilitary dress and that bloody great helicopter that is scaring the horses and dogs?"

"Sorry about the dramatic arrival and frightening the animals but we have come a long way across your land after a very unexpected discovery."

"I'm not sure what that could be, Kat, please come in for a cool drink and tell me more."

They were happy to move into the cool shade of the library and their first beers hardly touched the sides. Once Gloria had seen them settled, she left the room and returned a few minutes later accompanied by a very suave, cool, suited man, whom she introduced as her lawyer, who had stayed on after the ball.

"Hector will be as interested as I am to hear what you have to say."

It didn't take Ken and Kat long to describe what they had found on her property but they were circumspect about how they had come to look for it and why they and the authorities had made such a heavy handed intervention. Gloria affected amazement and appeared to take their story at face-value, but her lawyer was typically more forensic in his questioning about how they had suspected there was something amiss to find here and who was backing them. Then, as Gloria began to spin a story of innocence and complete ignorance about the presence of the Chinese in the signals station, she was interrupted by her personal aide who asked her to take a very important phone call. The lawyer accompanied her as she left the room and before Kat and Ken could kick back and relax their tired bodies, the Chef entered through another doorway and invited them with discreet hand gestures to follow him to his kitchen.

Having assured them that as Gloria's grandfather, he was devoted to her, he swore that he owed a higher loyalty and commitment to this country, that had made him what he was, rather than to a mythical motherland and its futile struggle to right its ancient grievances. Then he led them through the house to the tack room. They admired the array of bridles and saddles and as they were leaving, they could see the station camels being watered and ,one in particular, being scrubbed and rinsed clean of the country's heavy red dust.

In the lounge they found a much more subdued and pensive Gloria and when she left on the pretext of arranging for lunch. The lawyer who appeared equally deflated, confided that she had just received a call from the Prime Minister which seemed to have greatly disturbed her and almost reduced her to tears. With that he made his apologies and left to catch the station's plane back to Broome.

Half an hour later, they received an invitation to join Gloria in her personal, upstairs lounge. It was a very masculine den, furnished with red leather, Chesterfields, a huge mahogany desk, a picture of he who must have been her father above the open fire place and a brace of powerful rifles on a wall-mounted gun rack.

Gloria acknowledged their arrival with a curt nod and spoke in a quiet but firm tone.

"I have no intention of explaining any involvement I may have had in the activities you unearthed, and I certainly will not be apologising for my support for our greater ties with China."

Before she could draw breath and say more, Kat interrupted her.

"Gloria, we don't need you to either explain or even confess. We found these things in your tack room" and, holding up the boots and female riding clothes, caked in red dust, also, we saw your camel showing the signs of having been hard-ridden and covered in outback, road dust. At this moment we are sure that the security services are joining the dots regarding the picture of recent Chinese subversive activities, which we have exposed, and that their conclusions will find you at the centre of their financing and planning."

"I will not demean myself with any further dialogue with people of no consequence and no stake in the foundation of this country nor commitment to its glorious future in alliance with China. You may guess the nature of the Prime Minister's call and his advice regarding my future and so I have no need to justify myself to such nobodies. I do need, however, to recognise all you have done to frustrate my mission by ensuring your future ends here and now. I know that you are armed, and you must take out your firearms, very carefully, and lay them on the desk. Don't fool yourselves into thinking you can jump me because it would take me just a few seconds to pull the pin from the hand grenade I am holding and I have no fear of joining you in whatever eternity holds."

Ken was no expert in weaponry but the device she held looked convincingly lethal and her intention was not in doubt. They remained stock still as Gloria edged towards the door and it dawned on them that she was planning to escape and toss the hand grenade after her to blow them to bits. Her undoing was her high heeled sandals, which caught in the Turkish rug and threw her off balance. Before she had righted herself there was a powerful twang and she fell back, with a look of total unbelief, with a wicked cross bow quarrel protruding from between her breasts. She died slowly cursing and howling her rage against the pair as the Chef arrived, just in time to cradle her in his arms and kiss her goodbye.

Gloria had been unaware that the strap across Kat's shoulders supported her bow and even Ken didn't know that she had perfected a technique, allowing her to swivel the pre-loaded weapon and instantly release a deadly, underarm snap-shot.

28
FALLOUT

Canberra, ASIS Headquarters

"Kat and Ken, you have the heartfelt thanks of the government and the nation, for your brave actions in rooting out and putting a brake on the Chinese Communist Party's attempts to disrupt our way of life. Your undercover role achieved things that could not be done by our own officers and we wish you well as you return to your normal lives and careers. Rest assured we will keep you in mind and for a while resources will be committed to keeping you both safe from any reprisal action our opponents might try."

"Thank you minister. It has been a challenge and when we took on the assignment in Victoria, we had no idea of what it would grow into. We are pleased and proud of the outcome. Before we go, we would like to be assured that action is taken against some of the protagonists of CCP influence and that there is recognition and reward for those who helped us throw log jams in its path."

"Of course. I have asked George to do that, separately, when you have a debriefing meeting with him."

Richmond, Dinner at the Grand

"Hi K and K, back where we started, and where better to round things off and thank you for all you have done. We have rapped a few knuckles and others have been subject to the 'gypsy's warning' regarding excess Sinophilia. You will appreciate that much of what you did was undercover and not admissible in public. For this and for diplomatic reasons, we are unable to go in as hard as we would have liked but it's the result that counts. The CCP has lost tremendous face, there are rumblings of discontent below the leadership level at the over-reach of their bosses and their power-seeking strategies have either been thwarted, or at least set back, for the foreseeable future.

Complicit politicians, academics, scientists, Australian based Chinese business leaders and journalists, have had their fingers burnt and the worst offenders have suffered loss of wealth, position and employment and a lifetime embargo on government service and preferment. Some have had honours withdrawn and those who are not Australian citizens are quietly being encouraged to leave or being deported.

On the positive side of the ledger Jack, Den and myself have been honoured. Major Chow Lim has been promoted by his service and is held in high esteem by ASIS. Professor Charles Bright has been knighted by the British Government and is in line for the role of Chief Scientist. We have presented him with life membership of the MCC.

Major Lim's student collaborators have had their uni fees refunded and have been given extended work permits; not forgetting the reliable support work of Pete and his ex-British SAS mates, they have been granted, off-the-record, Australian, returned servicemen status, including all the benefits due to them and their wives, especially health coverage and pension rights.

The helpful Oceanographer, Wendy Wong, who helped expose the spy, has been awarded a substantial CSIRO research contract and the government is going to investigate the circumstances surrounding the suicide of the Victorian Chinese restaurant owners' son. It is certain that someone will be found liable for paying compensation and this will secure their economic future. Wombat has been offered a fault-free return to urban society or to remain in the bush with income and security guaranteed by the government.

All that remains is to thank and recognise you both, which for obvious reasons must remain under-wraps. But for you Kat, the government will ensure your parents get the best of aged and health service support, free of charge and as for you Ken, you will remain a legend within the service and you will always have the ear of the Prime Minister and the head of ASIS, the benefits of which are substantial but indefinable.

Thanks again and the least I can do is to pick up the tab for this superb spread. Cheers!"

29
EPILOGUE

Awake, Aware and Ready

Ken and Kat were back in Lygon street, enjoying the morning sun and relaxing over croissants and coffee outside a café, across from Ken's office. The traffic was light at that time of morning, which did little to hide the unmarked security service car, keeping watch against threats to K and K.

During the night they had made tender, farewell love in the knowledge that theirs was not a love match but rather an enduring friendship with the most trusted and cared for 'other' in their lives.

"It's good to be back Ken and lovely to relax and indulge in the little pleasures of life, on a morning like this, knowing that George is not going to disturb us and that the guys over there have our backs."

It's great Kat, but we have had so many surprises and faced so many dangers recently, I wonder what the future holds. Will life return to how we would like it, now that the CCP dragon has been slain, or are there new disruptions and dangers forming up just over the horizon?"

"Don't be so pessimistic. Enjoy the here and now, especially this tranquillity and state of peace. I must dash to catch a plane home. Kick back, order another coffee and enjoy a leisurely read of the Federation's special edition, which has lots of news and hopes about where we are going and Australia's immediate future. Go well and see you next time."

She kissed him, tenderly, shouldered her bag and swept out of the café

Ken took her advice. He ordered a strong Macchiato to help him focus and stay awake while he relished the sunshine and folded open the broadsheet and began to read, with growing interest and excitement.

"Yes. This is more like it and if Australia adopts many of these decisions and directions we will indeed survive and flourish in a tense and increasingly competitive and sometimes combative world."

THE FEDERATION

Established in Melbourne 1848 · 7 September 2022

AWAKE, AWARE AND FOREARMED

IN THIS special edition of the paper we cover developments that suggest Australia has woken from its complacent slumber and is taking vigorous steps to secure our internal and external security and ensure we continue free to prosper and enjoy our unique way of life in a land, distant from but engaged with the rest of the world.

PM: We have the will and we know the way!

LAST NIGHT the Prime Minister addressed the nation. He was forthright and passionate about our road ahead. This is what he said:

"My fellow Australians,

For some time, we have been asleep at the wheel and allowed complacency to ignore external threats and weaken our will and ability to resist them and face up to our internal challenges. This must change. Right now.

Parliament has approved a special budget which will significantly improve our readiness to secure and maintain our free and prosperous way of life, specifically, we will:

Significantly strengthen our security services and defence forces. Forge new alliances and strengthen existing ones with like-minded democracies which share our interests.

Overhaul the leadership and academic focus at our great universities. Welcome overseas students, but give preference to our own and discourage foreign interference.

Adoption and implementation of these new and exciting strategies will ensure a secure, free, prosperous and 'good-to-live-in', Australia."

More one than many

OUR IMMIGRATION policy is to be focused on diversity rather than division.

Australia will continue to embrace migrants from lands around the world, regardless of their ethnicity and religion, provided they meet the requirements of our skill, health and character expectations.

In addition to requiring commitment to obeying the laws and respecting prospective new citizens to demonstrate spoken and written fluency in English, they will have to adopt Australian values. This will be reinforced by gradually phasing out dual nationality rights.

Children, at school, will be encouraged to confirm their loyalty to Australia at all official functions.

Educated for life and work

FEDERAL AND state education ministers have met to map out the future of education in Australia and their proposals are:

- Focus education curricula heavily on subjects and skills vital to Australia's future development and continued prosperity
- Enhance teaching of western philosophy, cultural and political development
- Close TAFEs and outsource technical education to industry financed bodies – teaching what employers need and offering students secure and fulfilling lives and careers.
- Establish world class private (self-funding), technical and humanities teaching universities
- Close Confucius institutes
- Indian, other Asian and South American students preferenced over Chinese in Australia
- Embargo Chinese scientists from collaboration on Australian University research with Military applications.

DEFENDING US BY DAY AND NIGHT

THE DEFENCE Minister has released a new white paper that she said "Our forward strategies will enable our forces to defend the nation, regardless of the enemy, location, now and in future. Our priorities will be:

Strategic alliances

- Stronger defence ties with India, Japan, Indonesia, Taiwan, South Korea, Singapore
- Expanded defence ties with NATO and countries seceding from the dissolving EU — Germany, Holland, Poland, France, and Scandinavia (excluding Norway and Finland)

Defence equipment

- New submarines to be converted to nuclear propulsion, to match present and future enemy capabilities.
- Autonomous attack drones and Orca style, missile subs to patrol northern approaches and strategic seaways.
- Contingency planning to deploy defence missiles in the northern territory
- Defence technology collaboration with Five Eyes allies and Israeli scientists

Inter-operability

- Indian Ocean naval war exercises with India, UK, Singapore and Indonesia.
- Northern waters exercises with Japan, UK, South Korea, Singapore, Philippines, Taiwan and Vietnam
- Northern Territory, land exercises with US Marines, Indonesian special forces, Japanese and Singaporean troops.

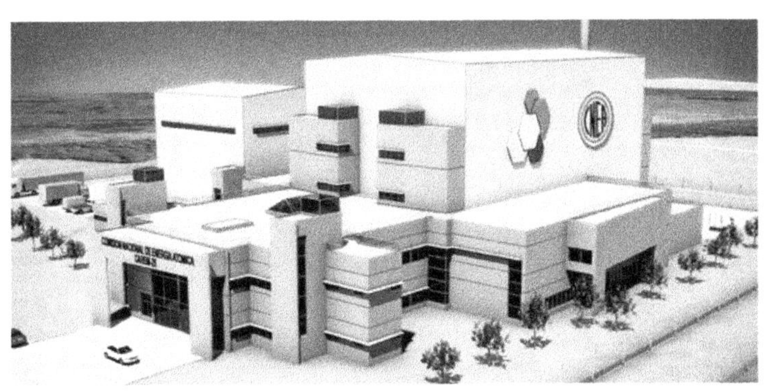

LIVING IN OUR (NUCLEAR) WORLD

AUSTRALIA will not pull up the drawbridge but will live in and trade with the world. We will:

- Be a full member of the G4 Anglo sphere technical and trade consortium (US, UK, Canada and NZ,) with India, Japan, Taiwan and Indonesia having associate status.)

- Accelerate development of a nuclear industries for peaceful purposes and trade uranium for know-how with our allies.

- Limit strategic mineral and energy exports to non-China/Russia allied countries.

ABOUT THE AUTHOR

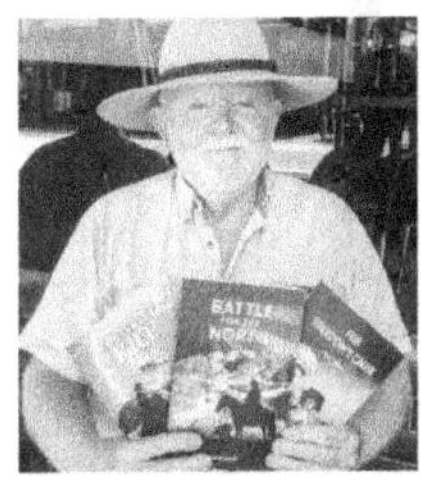 **Barry Smith** was born in England and educated in Manchester and at Cambridge University, where he read history. Australia has been home for over 50 years and he lives in marvellous Melbourne, where he is now living his dream of being a published writer.

Most of Barry's career has been in HR management and for 20 years before retirement he ran his own consulting business, focusing on turning around toxic management teams. Since retiring he has completed a doctorate focused on *"How I want to live and work in what's left of my life"* and over the past 10 years he has pursued dreams emanating from that—such as, crossing Siberia, touring Moorish Spain, finding his Manchester Regiment, Grandad's grave at Gallipoli, crossing USA by train and camp touring around Australia, carrying out research for and selling his Kimberley Trilogy of historical novels, in pubs and on outdoor markets from Cooktown to Broome and back.

You can follow Barry's further musings and adventures on Facebook at facebook.com/barrysmithwordspinner.

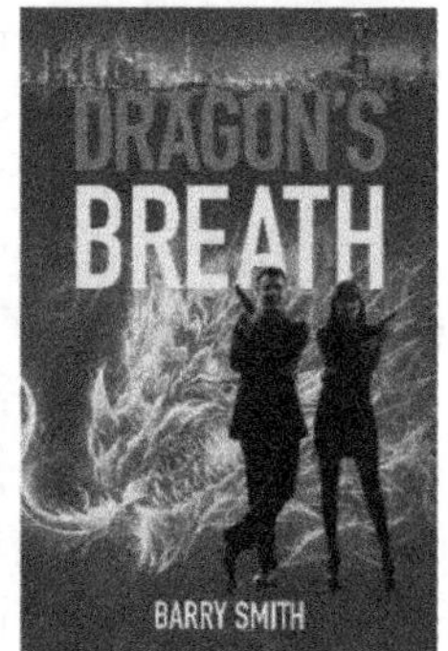

Where to get the books

Paperbacks and eBooks can be ordered online
from Amazon and from any major bookstore.

THE KIMBERLEY TRILOGY
Book 1

FOR FREEDOM'S CAUSE

For Freedom's Cause is a historical, romantic thriller set in England and Australia between the world wars. It follows the adventures and growing relationship between a working class English Army Officer, from Manchester — Dan Bevan — and a Melbourne barrister, serving with the Australian Light Horse — Charlie Elliott — who met, by chance, during the First World War and the strong women in their lives.

Having survived several of the major battles, both men are so disillusioned with the homes and occupations they return to, that Dan volunteers to suppress the republican rebellion in Ireland and Charlie joins an underground army to stand-up against mob riots in Melbourne. Despite their contrasting social origins and differing views on what form of government is best for preserving freedom and maintaining civil order, they become firm friends and when Dan is targeted by vengeful IRA assassins, he accepts Charlie's invitation to escape to Australia where he intends settling down peacefully in Melbourne, with the love of his life who unknown to him has born him a son.

When IRA gunmen pursue him from Melbourne to Perth he is forced to flee to a cattle station in the Kimberley where, finally reunited with his wife and son, he confronts his nemesis in that vast and mystical wilderness.

THE KIMBERLEY TRILOGY
Book 2

BATTLE FOR THE NORTH

Battle for the North reunites the heroes and heroines of *For Freedom's Cause* — Dan, Charlie, Elspeth Liza and Alice, in frustrating Japanese espionage plots and raids into northern Australia during World War 2. The action takes place in the Kimberley wilderness and celebrates the daring and heroism of mounted North Australian Observer Unit patrols, nicknamed the 'Nackeroos' or 'Curtin's Cowboys.'

Following on the bombing of Darwin and Broome, Japanese marine commandos land on the Kimberley coast to establish a foothold and deny the US and Australian Navies a secure re-fuelling and supply base. In the absence of Australia's regular forces in the Middle East and Singapore, all that stands between them and success is Dan Bevan's and Charlie Elliott's part-time observer patrols, which battle a Japanese special forces unit from Broome to their Kalumburu base and join the fight to push the enemy back into the sea.

Whilst Dan and Charlie conduct their guerrilla campaign in the bush, their wives and Lady Elspeth interrupt their war work in Darwin to hunt down a murderous Spy.

THE KIMBERLEY TRILOGY
Book 3

KIMBERLEY KILL

Kimberley Kill is the final novel in the trilogy. An international, religious war has broken out across the Middle East between Sunni and Shia Islamic sects, cutting off all energy supplies from that region. Frustrated by its inability to acquire sufficient energy to power its ever expanding economy, China has invaded Russia, annexing the Siberian oil and gas fields and precipitating World War 3. Cyber warfare has neutralised global defence communications creating a US-China stand-off and the only remaining operational satellite communication base in the Kimberley is threatened by invading Indonesian, special-forces. All that stands in their way is a small Norforce patrol backed by an Aboriginal tribe, whose female leader is intent on avenging the murder of her father, their Elder, and the desecration of their Wandjina guardian. Three strong minded and determined people — the devout Moslem leader of the Indonesian Kopassus force, the MIT trained daughter of an assassinated Aboriginal elder and the middle-aged, former SAS, gas platform engineer and part-time leader of the Norforce patrol — strive to contest and impose their conflicting beliefs and loyalties when they compete and clash in a hunt to the death across the harsh but beautiful Kimberley wilderness.

VICTORIA'S TWINS

The rise of Manchester and Melbourne
Tales of fighting for freedoms,
fortunes and football

This is a rich and dramatic historical novel that experiences the flowering of Manchester and Melbourne, two of the most significant cities of Queen Victoria's Empire, as they emerged and flourished during the turbulent years of the 19th and early 20th centuries.

Both gave birth to world famous, liberal leaning newspapers, *The Manchester Guardian* and *The Melbourne Age*, which referee the game through the astutely, forensic eyes of their most illustrious and campaigning editors, C.P. Scott and David Syme, but, who still can't help taking sides and entering the play.

It is in two parts.

Firstly, The Beginning Years, from 1854 to the start of WWI, follows the life and adventures of a former *Manchester Guardian* compositor who migrates to Melbourne in time to join *The Age*, as it reports the beginning of the Eureka rebellion and starts to comment on and shape the colony's and Australia's turbulent path to state and nationhood. With the constant oversight of Scott and Syme drawing out the similarities with Manchester's complementary fight for civil and political liberties and economic power.

Secondly, The Later Years relates experiences and escapades of a contemporary Manchester migrant, fleeing the dead hand of British socialism in the sixties only to land in the thick of Gough Whitlam's Prime Ministership and the gradual awakening of Melbourne from its prudish and censorial post war manacles to become the exciting cultural melting pot, and social, sporting and culinary pace-setter for Australia, that it is today.

As at many times in their histories, *The Guardian* and *The Age* are in serious, if not terminal, economic trouble, but their great powerhouse cities thrive and grow in the 21st century as never before.

KAT AND KEN ADVENTURE SERIES
Book 1

TERROR TRAILS

Australian secret agent Kat Douglas hits the ground running when she joins the secret state. Her grit is tested, her judgements questioned and her life threatened.

Can her fellow agent, Ken Eliot, depend on her when the going gets tough? Will he have her back? Can she trust him with her innermost secrets and her life?

Against a background of the unknown and feared, the pair battle terrorism, espionage, evil and much more. Questions of love, life, betrayal, and destiny confront readers, as they traverse the world with Kat and Ken, from Barcelona to St Petersburg and beyond.